RUBY·STARR

DEBORAH LYTTON

sourcebooks
jabberwocky

Published by Sourcebooks Jabberwocky, an imprint of Sourcebooks, Inc.
P.O. Box 4410, Naperville, Illinois 60567-4410
(630) 961-3900
Fax: (630) 961-2168
www.sourcebooks.com

Library of Congress Cataloging-in-Publication Data

Names: Lytton, Deborah A., author.
Title: Ruby Starr / Deborah Lytton.
Description: Naperville : Sourcebooks Jabberwocky, [2017] | Series: Ruby
Starr ; 1 | Summary: When a new fifth-grader, Charlotte, wants to turn
the lunchtime book club, The Unicorns, into a drama club, Ruby has to
use her imagination and love of reading to save the day.
Identifiers: LCCN 2016050823 | (alk. paper)
Subjects: | CYAC: Books and reading--Fiction. | Clubs--Fiction. |
Friendship--Fiction. | Schools--Fiction. | Imagination--Fiction.
Classification: LCC PZ7.L9959 Rub 2017 | DDC [Fic]--dc23 LC record
available at https://lccn.loc.gov/2016050823

Source of Production: Versa Press, East Peoria, Illinois, USA
Date of Production: June 2017
Run Number: 5009583

Printed and bound in the United States of America.
VP 10 9 8 7 6 5 4 3 2 1

For Ava and Caroline with love

CHAPTER 1

It All Begins with Books

*O*nce upon a time opens every fairy tale so it's the way I'm starting my own story. Once upon a time, there lived a girl named Ruby Starr. (That's me.) Here are some things you should know:

1. I love—absolutely, completely *love*—books (every kind of book, especially if it involves animals).
2. Pickles are my favorite food. (They go with everything. Even chocolate ice cream! Hmm, this is making me hungry...)

3. I say a lot of things without thinking (which sometimes gets me in trouble with a lowercase *t*).

4. The book that made me love books was *Harry Potter and the Sorcerer's Stone.* (Probably everyone says that, right?)

5. I have three besties—Siri, Jessica, and Daisy.

6. Sometimes I imagine I am in the pages of a book. My thoughts sort of fly up into bubble-gum bubbles full of ideas.

7. I believe in happy endings.

Today I'm not imagining things when my teacher, Mrs. Sablinsky, announces that we will be welcoming a new student to Room 15. (This is the way lots of books begin—with someone new coming to town.) I sit up a little taller in my seat and glance across the room at my best friend, Siri Mundy. Siri and I have been best friends since we were in kindergarten. Kindergarten to fifth grade is a lifetime. So we have been friends for something like forever. Siri raises her eyebrows and grins back at me. She just got braces, and they make her smile look even happier than usual.

I know what Siri is thinking. 'Cause I'm thinking the same thing. Someone new to join our Fearsome Foursome: Siri, Jessica, Daisy, and yours truly. (There's nothing really fearsome about us at all. I just like to say that because it sounds sort of superheroish.) Pink is our signature color. We use pink markers whenever possible, wear pink clips in our hair, and have pink laces in our sneakers. Even Siri's braces are pink. Confession time: I like green better than pink, but I got outvoted. So I wear the pink, but in my heart, I'm all about the green.

I watch the door all morning. It's not that

easy to write in cursive with my eyes looking up instead of down at my paper. But when a new character is about to step into the pages of a story, you don't want to miss it. I want to be the very first person in Room 15 to see who it is. Finally, the star-spangly door opens. She looks like she is already one of our group. She wears a pink headband in her smooth black hair, a floral skirt with a white tank top, and pink sneakers. She also looks sort of nervous, if you ask me. I think of all the books I've read about new kids, like Harry Potter, coming into a story. They always turn out to be the heroes. I'm not sure I like that.

"Class, this is Charlotte Thomas. Charlotte has just moved here from Northern California. I want everyone to welcome her and help her get settled in." Charlotte stands there quietly. But her eyes dart around the room. *Look at me, look at me!* I scream silently. Only her eyes skip right over me to land on Siri. I glance over at my best friend. Siri is smiling at Charlotte with her sparkly braces. Charlotte suddenly smiles back. And I can't believe my eyes. She has the same pink braces as Siri! Something in my stomach flips over right then. I know, somehow, that there is trouble ahead (maybe even trouble with a capital *T*).

So when Mrs. Sablinsky says, "Who would like to show Charlotte around and sit with her at lunch today?" I keep my eyes on Siri and raise my hand as fast as she raises hers. Only I must be faster, because Mrs. Sablinsky picks me. "Thank you, Ruby. I'm counting on you to make Charlotte's first day really special."

When Mrs. Sablinsky starts going over the schedule for the rest of the day, I begin imagining things.

I see myself walking Charlotte down a pink carpet. The other students stand along the carpet, taking photos of us like we are famous. The carpet leads all the way around school. Even Principal Snyder is waving to us. I wave back like a princess on parade. Only I don't see my glass slipper fall off. And I trip over it and tumble down the stairs, landing with a splash in a river of pickles.

"Ruby, did you have a question?" Mrs. Sablinsky's voice cuts into my imaginary world and drops me right back into the present. I want to say no, but my hand is waving back and forth in the air as though I have a very important question to ask. I don't want to embarrass myself, so I make one up, really fast. "What time is it in Paris?"

OK, it's not my best question. It's not even my sort-of-best question. It's lame. So I deserve the snickers and giggles. Even I want to giggle.

"Not amusing, Ruby." Mrs. Sablinsky does not have a sense of humor. I bet if a line of dancing goats came into the room right now wearing ballet tutus, she wouldn't even crack a smile. If you ask me, a sense of humor should be a requirement for teaching degrees. If I made the test for teachers, they would have to show that they can laugh at jokes and play charades. I'm positively one hundred percent certain that Mrs. Sablinsky hasn't ever played charades. (Charades is one of my top three favorite games:

1. Chess
2. Monopoly
3. Charades)

The class is still laughing at me. I look over at Siri and shrug. I pretend it's no big deal, but truthfully, I hate when people laugh at me. I love laughing. And I love jokes too. I just don't want to be one.

I keep my eyes on my work after that. I don't allow my mind to wander once. Then I hear the bell ring. Everyone around me scrambles out of their seats and runs for the door. I stand slowly and walk over to Charlotte. I don't want to seem too anxious. But Siri beats me there.

"Hi, I'm Siri," she says with a big smile.

"I'm Charlotte," the new girl returns with her matching grin.

"Hi, Charlotte, my name's Ruby, and I'll be your tour guide today," I say to remind them both that Mrs. Sablinsky picked me.

"Thanks for showing me around," Charlotte tells me as she stands up. She is exactly my height. Siri is a teeny bit shorter than both of us.

"You can eat lunch with us," Siri offers.

I was just going to say that. So instead, I show Charlotte where we keep our backpacks on the rack just inside the classroom. She hangs her purple-checked backpack on the hook at the end. I pull my lunch bag from the front pocket of my leopard backpack.

Siri grabs her lunch as well. She gets fun things like tamales and sushi. My lunches are not so inventive. I usually get a turkey or cheese sandwich with an apple. Charlotte holds a small bag of animal crackers and some grapes in her hand. I smile when Siri catches my eye. I know we are thinking the same thing again.

Sometimes our group shares lunch. And no one wants to share their something delicious with someone who has something not-so-delicious. Not-so-delicious foods include:

1. Broccoli
2. Bell peppers
3. Cauliflower

Not that I am anti-vegetable. I like vegetables just fine. After all, pickles are vegetables. I just don't like the gross ones.

I push open the door, and the sun makes me squint for a moment. Even in October, Southern California sun stays summer hot. "The fourth- and fifth-grade classes are all up here," I tell Charlotte, gesturing to the stairs that separate our classrooms from the rest of the campus. "And we have lunch together. We have to eat at the tables until the aide blows her whistle. *Woo-hoo.*" I demonstrate the sound so she'll know it when she hears it. "Then we can hang out until the bell rings." I think I'm a pretty good guide. I'm like a professional.

"It was kind of the same at my old school," Charlotte says. "Except there weren't any stairs."

"We can't cross back over these red lines until our teachers come to get us," I tell her, pointing to the wide red lines that circle the blacktop and lunch areas. I don't want to forget any important details. I am trying my absolute best.

"But if you forget your water bottle or something, you can ask one of the yard aides, and they will let you get it," Siri adds. I shoot her a look. This is *my* tour. I'm supposed to be giving Charlotte all the important information. Siri doesn't notice though. She is so gaga over Charlotte. It's like Charlotte is magical or something. (Sometimes this happens at the beginning of the book. The new kid puts everyone under a spell.)

"Did you have a best friend at your old school?" Siri asks.

Charlotte nods, and her big, blue eyes look round and sad. She doesn't say anything right away. I roll my eyes at Siri, who shrugs back at me.

"Rayna. She's going to visit me soon."

"That's great," I respond, trying to figure out a way to change the subject. But just then, Jessica and Daisy call out to us.

"We saved you seats!" Jessica and Daisy are squeezed onto the lunch benches at our usual table. At the other end sits a group of boys. We stay away from them, since they like to throw their food rather than eat it. And sometimes one of them will fake vomit on the table, just to watch everyone run away superfast. I take the end spot, farthest away from the boys and next to Daisy. I am not in the mood to be fake vomited on today. (Or any day to be exact. After all, who actually *wants* to be the star of a vomit scene?)

"You can sit here," I tell Charlotte. Siri is left to smush in between Jessica and one of the boys. She rolls her eyes at me. I mouth a *sorry* back to her. Siri shrugs. She shrugs a lot. It's her signature move.

"Did you ask her yet?" Daisy asks in between bites of her sandwich.

I try to signal her with my eyes. I open them real wide, telling her without words to wait. I'm not sure about Charlotte yet. Asking someone to join our group is a really big thing and not something I want to do so fast. I want to get to know her first. (In stories, it's always a mistake to trust the new kid too quickly, and I'm not going to fall into this trap.) Daisy doesn't seem to understand my eye language, or if she does, she decides to ignore me.

"About the Unicorns?"

It's too late. The word is already out there. Unicorns. Once someone hears a magic word like that, they never forget it.

"What are the Unicorns?" Charlotte asks. She offers Jessica one of her animal crackers. Jessica chooses a gorilla and makes him dance in the air before biting off his head.

"It's our book club," Siri answers helpfully. "Ruby started it."

Now all eyes are on me. I shrug, downplaying. "My mom's in a book club so I started the Unicorns. We meet once a week, at lunch."

"Right now we're reading *Black Beauty*," adds Jessica.

"Why Unicorns?" asks Charlotte. She holds the bag of animal crackers up to me.

I take one. Camel. Then I answer Charlotte. "Because they're magical creatures and you have to have an imagination to believe in them. Our book club is all about using your imagination." My voice sounds loud to me, and I can tell that I am frowning. I can feel it in my cheeks. I pop the camel into my mouth and bite down hard.

I imagine myself sitting at the lunch table with a book open in front of me. Suddenly, a unicorn climbs right out of the pages. She stands next to me, waiting for me to touch her pink horn so she can grant me one wish. I wish that I were the new girl in the story. Then I offer the unicorn a pretzel stick.

Someone nudges me in the side. I look up in surprise, expecting to see a unicorn. But instead, I see Daisy. Siri has just squeezed into the spot between Jessica and Daisy. I glance over at the boys. The food fight has already begun. They are pelting one another with grapes.

"When is your next meeting?" Charlotte asks Siri, who doesn't look at me once before answering.

"Tomorrow."

"Sounds like fun," Charlotte says. "Can I be a Unicorn too?"

This is my moment. My moment to speak up. It's not like I am the leader of the Unicorns or anything, but it was my idea and all. So I guess that makes me kind of the main Unicorn. But before I can think of something brilliant to say, Siri jumps in.

"Welcome to the Unicorns," she tells Charlotte. Charlotte grins at me. I smile back, but it feels kind of fake. I don't even show my teeth. My real smile is with teeth.

I twist the stem of my apple around, wishing I could stop time and rewind it. I want a redo on the last few minutes of my life. Now, I can think of a lot of things I could have said like, "We're in the middle of a book right now, so you can sit in tomorrow and observe."

My mom has taken me to lots of classes where I have observed the first time to see if I like them. I did that with art class, tennis, and even karate. Observing is like testing, so it's not a for-sure kind of thing. Or I could have said, "We take new members at the beginning of each month" or even, "We have a waiting list, so if you want to put your name down, we'll let you know when we have an opening."

But it's too late for all that. Because Siri is already pulling out her copy of *Black Beauty* and lending it to Charlotte. And Jessica is telling her to make sure to bring an extra-special lunch. Daisy even remembers to tell Charlotte to wear pink.

And just like that, we have a new member in the Unicorn Book Club. Whether I like it or not. (Fearsome Fivesome doesn't have a ring to it. Not at all.) But I don't say anything. Chapter 1 is written. Now all I can do is turn the page to Chapter 2.

Book Club Tuesday

I wake up with a stomachache. Usually Book Club Tuesday is my favorite day of the week. But not today. Today, I don't want to go.

"Mom! I'm not feeling well!" I call from my bed.

"I'll be right there," Mom answers.

I pull the covers up over my head, hoping for a fever. Maybe if I stay in here long enough, she'll forget about me.

My sheets turn into a cave made of deep-blue stone glittering with rubies. I'm hiding here to escape a giant who wants me to stay in his castle and cook his dinners of cauliflower and salmon, match up all the socks in his sock drawer, and feed his pet dragon, Huey. (Huey is kind of cute, but he eats live cockroaches.) I hear the giant calling my name, but I don't answer.

Suddenly, the sheets are pulled back. I expect to see the giant. But instead I see my mom. She doesn't smell like cauliflower or salmon. She smells all fresh and clean like a spring day. She's wearing a gray shirt and black pants, which means workday. I can always tell where Mom will be each day, at work or at home, because of her clothes. Her work clothes are serious black and gray officey-looking shirts and skirts. Her home clothes are jeans with printed, flowy shirts, all bright and cheery. I personally prefer the home clothes to the work clothes, because I'm more about color than black and white.

"What's wrong, Ruby?" Mom asks as her hand touches my forehead. "You don't feel warm to me."

"It's my stomach," I moan. I'm not acting—not really. It does hurt a lot. There are three things I can't stand:

1. Stomachache.

2. Not getting enough sleep. (You know that feeling when your eyes don't want to open, and it's like you're ungluing them each time you try to blink? I really hate that. I know *hate* isn't a nice word to say, but I think it's OK when I am just talking about eyelids, and they happen to be my own.)

3. Itches. (Itches are just so itchy!)

I see myself hunched over with a stomachache and scrunching my face to try to unglue my eyelids. At the same time, I am scratching an itch on my ankle. No wait, on my elbow. Now on my back. Arggggggggh! I limp forward, scratching and blinking right up the steps of school. Only I look like a prehistoric creature squelching out of a tar pit. Definitely not hero material! Can anyone say, "Run!"?

"Ruby?" Mom stops my hand from scratching the imaginary itch. (Or maybe it's not imaginary because now it's moved to the back of my knee. How do itches move around so fast?) "Maybe you're hungry?" Mom tries to help. She brushes my curls away from my face. My hair is blond and curly. And when I wake up, the curls are wild and crazy. My bedhead makes me look like a lion in the morning. (*Roar!*)

"I don't think so," I say. This isn't going the way I hoped. I wanted her to say I could stay home right away.

"This is book club day. You don't want to miss that. And I made you a special lunch for talking about *Black Beauty*." Mom picks up my clothes from the chair where I laid them out last night. She carries them to the bed. I sigh.

Mom's emerald-green eyes meet mine. Our eyes are the exact same color. Sometimes looking into her eyes is like looking into a mirror.

"Ruby, is there something going on at school? Some reason you don't want to go today?"

Three reasons:

1. Charlotte

2. The Fearsome Fivesome

3. Book Club. All of which are actually really the same reason: Charlotte.

I shrug. Nothing has happened. Nothing that I can explain anyway. It's just a feeling. And having a feeling isn't enough reason to stay home from school, at least not in my experience.

"Do you want to talk about it?" Mom asks. She sits down next to me on my bed and holds my hand.

I shake my head. "It's nothing really. I don't even know why my stomach hurts. Maybe I'm coming down with something."

"Maybe you are," Mom says. "Why don't you

get dressed and have some breakfast, and then we'll see if you feel any better."

"OK," I agree. I hadn't really expected to stay home, but it was worth a try. And I don't know what I'm so afraid of anyway. It is my book club after all.

I see myself standing in front of school, wearing green armor and carrying a purple shield with a picture of a unicorn on it. I am armed not with a sword but with a book. I am a symbol of bravery and courage. I will fight for my beliefs. I will fight for books.

I put on plaid shorts and a white T-shirt. Then I slip on my green sneakers with the pink laces. After brushing my teeth and pulling my hair into a ponytail, I'm ready.

★ ★ ★

Breakfast in our family isn't like in TV commercials where all the family sits down together and eats at the same time. There are five of us—my mom, my dad, two brothers, and me. I'm the youngest. My brother Connor is thirteen, and Sam is fifteen. They almost never sit down to eat, except for family dinners. Dad leaves early for work, so he's usually waving good-bye right around the time I bite into my pancakes.

Today, it's the usual. Everyone is going in different directions, kind of like my hair.

Mom hands me a plate with toast and eggs. I don't feel up to this much food, but I take it to the table without a word.

"Grandma is picking you up today," Mom tells me. "I have to stay a little late at work, so I won't be home until dinnertime. You can fill me in on the book club then. How is your tummy feeling now?"

When my mom says *tummy*, it's like she has forgotten that I am ten. It's like she still thinks I am three years old and in love with Elmo. (Right now, if Elmo sang his happy song to me, I would probably throw some toast at him.)

I shrug. "Better, I guess." It isn't really better. It's still churning around like I have just ridden an upside-down roller coaster after eating cotton candy and ice cream. But I know I'm not really sick, just nervous.

★ ★ ★

The nervous feeling stays all morning, and by lunch, I have decided that I will make the best of it. Everyone else seems to like Charlotte. And truthfully, I like her too. Maybe my stomachache was a real stomachache after all, and not a worrying stomachache.

We all gather at our usual table. Two on one side and three on the other. I'm on the two side, next to Jessica. I open my lunch bag and pull out my napkin. Mom always sends me a big cloth napkin on Tuesdays. I open it up and spread it on the table in between us.

"We share our lunches on Tuesdays," I explain to Charlotte. "It makes it more book-clubbish that way."

One by one, we all set our food out on the napkin. Mom has packed me special sandwiches with cream cheese and cucumber, cut into little hearts. I also have grapes and chocolate-chip cookies. Siri shares her mini taquitos and straw-berries. Jessica adds a peanut butter and jelly sandwich and orange slices. Daisy has brought pizza bites with trail mix, and Charlotte has a turkey wrap, pretzels, and a giant brownie. There is a lot of excitement over the brownie. It annoys me that they like her brownie more than my cookies.

"We eat while we discuss the book," Siri tells Charlotte as she grabs a pretzel.

"I didn't get a chance to read it last night," Charlotte admits.

"That's all right," Daisy tells her. "You can just listen this time."

"Is anyone finished with the book?" I ask first. We always check to see if someone hasn't finished because we don't want to spoil the ending.

I glance around at my friends. They are all stuffing brownie into their mouths. Their teeth are turning brown like they've been brushed with mud instead of toothpaste. Kind of unappetizing if you ask me, but no one is asking me. Siri, Daisy, and Jessica shovel more brownie before shaking their heads, *no*.

No one has finished the book. No one, that is, except *moi*. (That's French for *me*.) I don't speak French, but I pick things up in books I read. Words in French like *moi* and *arrivederci* in Italian. (That's *good-bye*. I think it sounds happier than the English way. Less like good-bye and more like *see ya soon*).

"I am," I tell them. "But don't worry." I zip my lips closed, turn the key, and toss it over my shoulder.

"Do you think Black Beauty's mother gives him good advice?" I ask, taking a bite of one of Mom's cucumber sandwiches.

"She wanted him to be a good horse for his owners," Siri says.

"I think she wanted to be proud of him," Jessica adds.

"I think she would have been proud of him," I say. "I think he was the most wonderful horse that ever lived."

"He's not real, you know," Charlotte says with a roll of her eyes. "He's just a character in a book."

Confession time: I hate it when people remind me that characters in books aren't real. They are real to the authors who write them. And they are real to the readers (like me) who love them. So telling me that they aren't really real just makes me want to growl.

"I know that," I tell her, with a big eye roll of my own. "But the author made him seem real—that's what I meant." I glance over at Siri. *What do you think of your new girl now?* I say with my eyes.

Siri shrugs. "I thought it was sad that he had to leave his mother and his meadow."

"His life was good and then bad," Daisy adds. "I liked his friend Merrylegs."

"Ginger's not so nice though," I comment, with a look at Charlotte.

"But Black Beauty sees something in her, and I think they become friends because no one else has given her a chance before." Siri eats a little piece of cucumber sandwich.

I don't think Siri is speaking about Black Beauty anymore. She's speaking about Charlotte.

"At my old school, my friends and I played this really fun game." Charlotte changes the subject suddenly. Talking about another subject at a meeting is a book club no-no. But Charlotte doesn't know this. She pulls all the attention away from *Black Beauty*. Everyone looks at her.

"What was it?" Jessica asks.

"We made up our own plays," she announces with a giant sparkly smile. "And then acted them out."

"I want to do that!" Siri practically jumps out of her seat with excitement.

"Me too!" Daisy claps her hands together.

"We can make one up today," Charlotte says.

"But we're in the middle of book club," I remind them. I look at Siri for help, but she is smiling her matching smile at Charlotte.

"Jessica?" I look at the only other person in the group who loves reading as much as I do.

"We've already talked about *Black Beauty*," Jessica tells me in a small voice.

"Not really," I argue. "We've only talked about

the beginning. What about his friendships?" And my friendships, I think.

Charlotte stands up. "Is there someplace we have more room?" she asks Siri.

"We have to wait for the aide to blow the whistle," I remind them. I sound a little like Mrs. Sablinsky. And that's not a good thing. Only just then the aide blows the whistle.

Siri looks at me quickly and then looks away. "We can go by the four square courts. I'll show you."

This can't be happening. I must be in the middle of a nightmare. Because I can't actually be sitting here, watching my friends leave a book club meeting before it's finished. But it's happening. My friends hurry to clean up their lunches, shoving half-eaten food into their lunch bags.

"You coming?" Jessica asks.

"I'll be there in a minute," I tell her. But I'm not sure I will be there at all. I'm not sure I want to. This is Book Club Tuesday after all. Now

I understand the feeling in my stomach. It was warning me that everything was going to change. I really wish I had stayed home in bed.

I see myself sitting underneath a shady tree in a meadow. Black Beauty grazes on the grass nearby. Ginger and Merrylegs munch on apples that have fallen off the tree. "I will never leave you, Beauty," I promise. Black Beauty lies down next to me. Suddenly, an apple drops from the tree and hits me in the forehead.

"Ouch!" I rub my head. Only I'm not in the meadow, but at the lunch tables. I'm being pelted with pretzels. Tears fill my eyes, without my permission. Ruby Starr Rulebook: Do not cry at school. Ever. Not even if your best friends leave you alone at the lunch tables. Not even if you forget your homework and your teacher yells at you in front of the entire class. Not even if a ball hits you in the face during dodgeball.

So I rub the back of my fist over my eyes.

"Sorry, Ruby. We didn't mean to hit you," I look up and see Will P standing there. We have two Wills in our class. Will B drools and likes to pick his nose and eat it. (No comment.) And Will P wears supercool red glasses and sometimes makes me laugh with his funny jokes. He's all right, I guess (for a boy anyway).

It's Will P who is saying *sorry* to me.

"Where are your friends?" he asks me. "Isn't today your book club meeting?"

I guess even boys know about our book club. I shrug, feeling my eyes getting watery on me again.

"Ruby!" I look up to see Siri calling to me from across the yard. She waves at me to come with her.

I stand up. Will's hair has pretzels sticking out of it. I can't help but smile. "We ended early today. We're making up a play or something."

"Too bad you only let girls read books with you. I like to read," Will tells me.

"Maybe you should start your own book club," I say. Then I glance back at the table of boys. The yard aide has stopped the food fight.

"Great. I told those guys we'd get in trouble." Will P turns to go.

"You might want to start with the pretzels in your hair," I offer.

Will's mouth opens in surprise. Then his cheeks turn red. I point to the pretzels, and he feels around for them. He yanks them out and then holds them in the air for me to see. Will taps the pretzels together like drumsticks.

Will P is known for two things:

1. Everybody likes him—seriously, everybody. Even the mean substitute teachers smile at him.

2. His signature sock collection. Will P has all these different kinds of socks. I can't even imagine where he gets them. He has socks with animals like zebras and sharks, socks with trash like crushed cans and fish bones, socks with soccer balls and basketballs, even socks with instruments. Today he is wearing socks with dogs all over them. There are poodles and collies, beagles and golden retrievers. I think I even spot a pug.

"I like your socks today," I tell him.

"Thanks!" he calls back as he walks away.

I sit there alone. I hope the bell will ring and save me from joining Charlotte's play. I count to 540, and still the bell doesn't ring. So I take my lunch bag and drop it into my class basket. And then I take the smallest steps possible across the yard to the four square courts.

"You OK?" Siri asks me right away.

"I guess," I tell her. How OK can I be when my Book Club Tuesday has just turned into Queen Charlotte's Tuesday?

"Ruby, we already picked parts. Siri is going to be the princess. I'm her mother, the queen. Daisy is our horse trainer, and Jessica is our fairy godmother. Do you want to be Siri's sister?" Charlotte is quite the director. She has it all figured out already.

"Sure." I don't really care which part I play.

"Siri and you both want to go to the ball.

But only one of you can go. So I have to choose one of you. You have to dance your best dance for me to choose."

Here are the things I like to do: I read, I write, I play piano. I can even ride a horse. Here are the things I cannot, will not do: I. Do. Not. Dance.

"Um, not sure about the dancing thing," I start to say. But Charlotte isn't paying attention to me anymore. She is demonstrating a dance move. Spinning. Charlotte spins around and around and around. She spins so many times I think she might take off into the air. My friends start clapping. They actually stand in a line watching Charlotte show off. And they clap for her.

Before anyone can notice my bad attitude, the bell rings. I am saved. Or so I think.

Because I think my day can't possibly get any worse. But I am wrong—so very, very wrong.

CHAPTER 3

Not Thinking Pink

Quiet down, Room 15," Mrs. Sablinsky tells us as soon as we take our seats. "I have some exciting news. Today, we are starting a new project—and it's my favorite one of the year. You will be creating a drawing of the Statue of Liberty, with a factual paragraph below. Do your research, and tell me something I don't know about Lady Liberty."

Mrs. Sablinsky begins handing out the assignment sheets. She continues talking. "We'll be working on this for the next week or two, so you will have plenty of time to make your projects extra special."

I love working on projects like this. I'm not a super-great artist or anything, but I can use my imagination. And any schoolwork that involves imagination doesn't feel like work at all.

"You will work in pairs. So go ahead and choose a partner now."

I look across the room at Siri. We always pair up on class projects. But she is looking in the other direction. So I hurry over to her.

"Hey, partner," I say to the back of her head. Just then I see Charlotte. She is already sitting beside Siri. It can't be. Siri would never do that to me. Would she?

Siri turns then and looks at me. Her brown eyes are wide underneath her long bangs. "Sorry, Ruby. Charlotte asked me first. And since she's new…" She trails off. I don't know what the end of the sentence is. *And since she's new, I thought I would be nice and partner with her.* Or, *And since she's new and interesting, I wanted to partner with her instead of boring old you.* I'm thinking it's the second one. But it doesn't really matter, because Siri isn't going to be my partner for the first time since kindergarten. Maybe that isn't a big deal to Siri, but it's a really, really big deal to me.

"OK," I mumble. Not, OK like "I'm OK with it." But OK like "What else can I do?"

I look around the room. Jessica and Daisy are already paired up. There are a few other girls in class I wouldn't mind working with—like Hazel and Molly, but they seem to be paired up too. While I have been wasting time talking to Siri, I have missed my chance to get a good partner.

Mrs. Sablinsky notices me standing there. Partnerless. (For those who have never experienced this horrific state, let me explain what it's like. It's like standing in the middle of class in your underwear with everyone staring.)

"Ruby, do you need a partner?"

It's pretty obvious. Why do teachers have to

ask obvious questions when they already know the answers? Is it so they can make us think they need our help when we really don't?

"Yes, Mrs. Sablinsky," I say. For the first time, the answer is *yes*.

"Will doesn't have a partner either. You can work with him," she tells me as she hands me a poster-size piece of paper.

"Thank you," I say as I look around for Will. It's not so bad to work with him. He's probably the top student in class, and he does make me laugh. It's not the same as working with my BFF though.

I spot Will on the other side of the room and hurry toward him. My paper flaps back and forth in my hands like it wants to fly in the air. I can't wait to get started. I have so many ideas.

Will is sitting at his desk. But I notice he already has a partner, one of the pretzel throwers, Bryden.

"Mrs. Sablinsky said you needed a partner,"

I tell him. Now I am really confused. And I am wasting more time.

Will shakes his head. "Not me, Will B."

The worst rhyme in rhyming history.

Will B? Will B! The Will who drools on his desk? Who picks his nose and then eats it? Who burps in the middle of music class? *This is my partner?*

I turn to look at the first desk at the front of the room. And there he sits, picking his nose. I watch in horror as he wipes his booger-covered finger underneath the desk. EWWWWWWWWWWWWWWWWWWWWW WWWWWWWWWWWWWWWWWWWW! Silent reminder to self: never, ever under any circumstances ask to move to Desk One.

I look back at Siri, who is happily drawing with Charlotte. She has no idea who I have to work with now, thanks to her.

I go to the front of the room and sit at the

desk next to Will B. I think this is Jessica's desk so it is safe to sit here. It's germfree and all.

I set the paper down on the desk. It flutters as I smooth it down, like it doesn't want to be still. I don't want to be still either. I want to yell and scream and run right out of this classroom.

The paper turns into a white dragon with emerald eyes and
scales that flicker rainbow colors. The class screams in fear,
all hiding underneath their desks. Even Mrs. Sablinsky hides.
But not me. I am not afraid. I climb on the dragon's back,
and we fly away. We fly to an island of dragons. I become
their queen. Queen Ruby, they call me.

"Ruby, what do you want to draw first?" I realize it's Will B calling me and not dragons. I sigh and answer him.

"The face, I guess. Let's draw the face."

★ ★ ★

The rest of the day is spent working on the project with our partners. Truth is, Will B is kind of smart. And he's a supergood artist. I think we might actually get a good grade on our project. But I'm still mad—not steam-coming-out-of-my-ears mad like on a cartoon, just sort of growling mad.

The Unicorns always walk out of school together. It's our thing. But today, we walk out with Charlotte too. One more thing that's different.

I am really happy when I see my grandmother waiting for me.

"Gram!" I call out. Then I run to her and hug her tight.

"Hi, sweetie pie. How was your day?" She

takes my backpack from me and puts it over her shoulder. Mom does the same thing. But it looks really out of place on Grandma. Not that grandmas can't sport leopard, but mine seems more like a flower backpack girl. She has short, light-blond hair and green eyes exactly like mine and Mom's. Gram loves playing golf and jogging. I can't imagine anything worse than jogging for fun. (Especially if you get that pain in your side. You know the one—it sort of pinches on one side of your stomach after you have to run at school. For sure, running is definitely not high on the fun meter.)

"Horrific," I tell her in one word. One word that sums up the entire day.

"We have time for an ice cream before we pick up your brothers. Everything looks better over ice cream," she suggests.

I glance over my shoulder to see Siri and Charlotte playing a clapping game—the same clapping game that I taught Siri last week. I force myself to look away.

Mom went back to work three years ago. Since then, Gram picks us up once or twice a week when Mom works late. So Gram exchanged her sensible senior car for a sporty SUV. She got a personalized license plate, GRAMBUS. She thinks it's cute, but it's slightly embarrassing for me and my brothers. She makes it even more embarrassing when she adds bunny ears sticking up from the hood of the car at Easter time and a fluffy tail to the trunk. At Christmas, she gives Grambus a Rudolph makeover with antlers and a red nose in the front.

Since it is mid-October, she has already dressed her car for Halloween. There are two black triangles and a giant black smile attached to the hood. Against the white of the car, the black face looks kind of like a ghostly Cheshire cat. "Grambus is ready for Halloween," I comment.

"You like it?" Gram asks.

I nod. I really do like it, even if it is a tad noticeable. "Especially the smile. Your car is a giant, happy pumpkin."

"That's the idea," Gram answers. I climb into the backseat and buckle up. Gram drives us to Ice-Cream Heaven. It's my favorite.

I don't talk much. I just let Gram tell me about her dog, George, and his latest adventures. Abe and George are our dog brothers. We got the puppies at the same time. Abe lives with us, and George lives with Gram and Grandpa. They both love to get messy. If there is a muddy puddle on the ground, they will roll in it. (Important fact: Abe and George are labradoodles, which are half Labrador retriever and half poodle.)

"This morning, George decided to help your grandfather put the groceries away. And he ripped apart three rolls of toilet paper before your grandfather noticed. When I came into the room, it looked like George was lying in a mound of snowflakes." Gram laughs. I can't help but laugh with her, even though I am still mopey.

"What did Grandpa say?" I ask her, even though I already know the answer.

"What he always says: 'G-E-O-R-G-E!'" Gram makes her voice really deep and loud.

Gram parks in front of Ice-Cream Heaven, and we go inside. The whole place is painted blue like the sky with white puffy clouds. There are round seats and little gold tables to sit at and eat ice cream. My favorite part is that the ice cream comes in clear pink bowls with tiny pink spoons that change color from pink to purple when they get colder. So you dip a pink spoon into the ice cream, and a purple spoon comes out. Plus, they have my number one favorite flavor here. Chocolate-chip caramel.

"The usual?" Gram asks.

I nod. Words aren't necessary when you know

someone really well. And Gram knows me better than anyone.

"A scoop of chocolate-chip caramel with a waffle cone on the side and a cloud topping, please," Gram orders for me. (The cloud is really just whipped cream, but they call it a cloud on account of the theme.)

The girl behind the counter hands me the pink bowl with my chocolaty ice cream and fluffy whipped cream. On the side is a waffle cone. I like to break off pieces and dip them in the ice cream. I lift out the pink spoon. It's half-purple already.

Gram orders a vanilla soft serve in a cone. After she pays, we sit down at one of the tiny tables. Different sizes of wings are painted all over the top of the table. I set my bowl down in the center of a pair of silver wings. So it looks like the bowl can fly away at any moment.

"Hang on to that ice cream," Gram teases.

I manage a half smile at her. Suddenly, I'm not so hungry. Turns out even ice cream can't make you feel better when your heart is broken.

"Want to tell me about the horrific stuff now?" Gram asks.

I take a long, deep breath.

And I tell her the whole story.

Gram doesn't say a single word the entire time. She doesn't even lick her ice-cream cone. She just listens. She's great at listening. She's probably the best person I know when it comes to listening. She's even better than Abe (even though he's not exactly a person, since he's a labradoodle).

"That does sound pretty horrific," she says when I finish. Then she eats her ice-cream cone. I eat my ice cream too.

"I don't even want to wear pink anymore," I admit. "Maybe I'll change my laces to a new color." Only one choice comes to mind. Blue. Sad blue.

"I bet it hurt you a lot to see your friends walk away from your book club like that," Gram tells me.

I nod. If I say another word, tears are going to dribble out of my eyes. I blink them in.

"It's kind of like George and a new toy," Gram continues. "Whenever I bring a new toy into the house, he completely forgets about all his other toys, even his favorite, a raggedy old bunny. He leaves that bunny behind, and the new toy is the best thing in the world. For that day. Because by the next morning, the new toy is underneath the sofa with all the other toys, and he's carrying his bunny around, just like before."

"I'm a raggedy old bunny?" I am a bit offended by Gram's comparison.

She laughs. "Not my point. Let me try again."

I lean on my elbows and listen really hard.

"Ruby, you have known your friends since kindergarten. Yesterday, they met someone new, and they thought she was exciting and different. Maybe you did too."

I shake my head.

"Even a little?" Gram grins sideways at me. I have to smile back. I can't help myself.

"I don't want to smile, but your smile is making me," I tell her.

That makes her smile more. "I'm sure it was hard for her to start a new school in the middle of October. Maybe she can be your friend too," Gram suggests.

I roll my eyes. "If I learn to sing and dance by lunch tomorrow."

"Ruby, just be yourself. Always be you." Gram kisses me on the top of my head.

Always be me.

Inspiring words. But then again, Gram doesn't have to dance on the playground just to stay in the play.

I see myself on the playground. It is my turn to perform.
Only suddenly, I have turned into a tin girl. I am completely
made out of tin. I can't bend my arms or legs or even turn
my head. All I can do is swivel around on one foot. The
Unicorns, along with the entire school, stare. And then they
start to laugh at me. I begin to cry, and I rust myself.

★ ★ ★

By the time my brothers climb into the car, I have decided three things:

1. The new character isn't always a hero.
2. Bad days really do get better with ice cream.
3. I need to learn to dance in one night.

CHAPTER 4

Is *Worser* Even a Word?

I have practiced piano and finished my homework by the time Mom gets home. Tuesday nights, we have math and science. Then we are supposed to read, but I read every night anyway. I read right before bed because that way, I dream about the stories, and they sort of become a part of me.

We are all in the kitchen. Me, Gram, Connor, and Sam. Sam and Connor are still working on their homework. I'm trying to set the table around them.

Gram has started dinner, two kinds of pasta with three different sauces. No one in my family eats the same. Mom is a vegan, Dad is gluten-free, Sam likes to have meat in every meal, Connor doesn't do sugar, and me—I eat everything. So Gram has made a regular fusilli (the squiggly kind) and a gluten-free spaghetti. The three sauces are: plain tomato, tomato with meat sauce, and parmesan and olive oil with veggies. "That way, there's something for everyone," she tells me.

"I'd make my family eat the same thing," I tell her. "I wouldn't make three different meals three times a day. That's nine meals every single day and sixty-three meals a week—not even counting snacks and desserts. If you add those, you might as well open a restaurant."

Gram chuckles at that. "Your mom and your aunt never ate anything the same. So I always had to make at least two meals for every meal. Your grandfather was easy. Like you. No food issues."

"I like it all," I tell her proudly. And Gram lets me taste the sauces one by one. They are all good, but the plain tomato is my favorite. "Maybe I'll put all three on my pasta," I tell her.

"How do you spell *arachnophobia*?" Connor asks.

"A-r-a-c-h-n-o-p-h-o-b-i-a." Gram is a spelling whiz.

"What does that mean?" I want to know.

"Fear of spiders," Connor answers without looking up. "I have to write a paper about my family."

"Who are you describing?" Sam asks as though he already knows the answer.

"You!" Connor, Gram, and I all shout at once.

Sam doesn't look amused. "You're not reading this to the class, right?"

"Worried much?" Connor answers. Sam just rolls his eyes and turns back to his history reading. Sam is my super-sporty brother. He plays soccer, baseball, tennis, volleyball, and basketball. I think he's best at baseball, but he likes basketball the most. He's really into eating healthy and being fit so he's really strong and muscly. But if he sees a teeny, tiny spider crawling across the floor, he starts screaming like he's seen a ghost. (Not that seeing a ghost is scary—not for me anyway. I've never seen one, but I've read about them in a lot of books. Sometimes they are really friendly.)

Connor, on the other hand, loves spiders and lizards—anything he can catch and observe. Connor is really into studying things. Mom says he will be a famous scientist some day and invent cures for diseases and stuff. I think he'd be a really amazing teacher because he loves learning, and he can explain things really well.

Abe lifts his head off the floor and makes a little crying sound. Then he goes to the back door and wags his tail.

"Mom's home," I announce. Abe is better than a telephone. He always lets us know what is happening. One time, he even told us the stove was on. He just kept barking and barking. And then Mom came into the kitchen and realized she had left it turned on by mistake. Abe is smart like that.

Mom opens the door seconds later. I run over and wrap my arms around her middle. And then I hug her supertight. I really needed to see her today. Just holding on to her makes me feel a lot better.

"Hi, sweetie. How was your day? Mmm, smells good in here. Thanks for starting dinner for me, Mom. That was really thoughtful of you." Mom strings sentences together when she's tired.

She kisses Gram on the cheek, then walks over to Connor and Sam and drops kisses on their heads too. I'm still hanging on to her waist. She just carries me along with her. Abe follows behind us, wagging his tail and trying to jump on Mom.

"Let me just change out of my work clothes, and I'll take over," she tells Gram. I let her go then, but only after she hugs me tight. "I want to hear all about book club as soon as I get back."

Gram and I look at each other at the exact same moment. And it's like we can read each other's minds. I have always wanted to be able to read minds. Right now, I can tell that Gram is telling me it will be OK. I wish it would be OK, but somehow, deep in my heart, I know today was only the beginning of something that will only get worser and worser, if that's even a word. (If it isn't a word, it should be. The people who put words in the dictionary should include *worser* if it isn't already in there, because there is nothing better to describe something that's even worse than worse.)

★ ★ ★

Dad is home by the time we sit down together. Dinner is the one time we are all at the same place at the same time.

"*Bonsoir, ma petite fille,*" he says to me. And then to Mom, "*Le dîner est merveilleux.*"

Dad is studying French from these CDs he listens to in the car. He doesn't need to learn it for work or anything. He just likes to learn new things for fun. Last year he taught himself how to sculpt ceramics, like bowls and vases. Our kitchen shelves are packed with his designs. This year, he decided to learn a new language. He practices on us at dinner. Since none of us speak French (except me with my one word, *moi*), we have no idea what he is saying. But he sounds good anyway.

"Did you finish the new story?" Mom asks him as she serves herself tomato sauce on fusilli, same as me.

"As a matter of fact, I did. And the producers loved it. They're running it tomorrow."

Dad is a news writer for our local morning news show. He writes the special interest pieces.

"The one about the parents who started their own school?" Connor asks.

"One and the same," Dad answers, thankfully in English so we can understand him.

"Maybe you should start a school," I suggest. "I can be your first student."

The school looks like a castle made out of silver. I am the
first student to be welcomed to the campus. I walk across a
rainbow bridge where I am greeted by my parents. I am the
only student in the school. Well, the only human student
anyway. I am followed by dragons, unicorns, fairies, elves,
and even a golden lion.

"Earth to Ruby," my brother Sam is saying.

"Sorry," I mutter. "I didn't hear you."

Mom is watching me. She looks worried. I can tell by the way her eyes are focused on me. It's like she is trying to see inside, to see how I feel. "Not good today?" she asks.

"Worse than not good. Worser even," I answer.

"I'm not sure that's a word," Sam tells me.

"Me either, but it should be," Dad responds as he reaches over and pats my arm.

"I need to learn how to dance," I admit.

"That's a great idea," Mom answers. "I know there's a nice dance studio near the high school."

"By tomorrow," I finish.

"Tomorrow!"

"Good luck with that," Connor says.

"Dancing does not exactly run in the Starr family," Sam adds.

"Boys, please," Mom says in her mom voice.

That's the voice that means business. The boys shrug and finish their dinners.

"We can work on something after dinner," Mom offers.

"I might be able to help," Dad says with a grin.

Not likely. But I know how I feel when my brothers tease me. So I don't say anything jokey. I just smile.

★ ★ ★

After dinner, Connor and Sam do dishes with Dad. Mom and I head to the living room. I explain to Mom about the book club and the play and everything. Then I tell her that Gram told me to be myself. But myself is a non-dancing, non-singing girl.

"Everyone can dance, Ruby. We just have to help you feel the beat. That's all."

I don't want to look like one of those oddball grandmas in cartoons who try to dance and look completely wacky. "Just don't let me make a fool out of myself," I beg her.

"The easiest thing for you to do is make up a routine where you step forward and back and side to side. Maybe spin once or twice. That should do it."

She makes it sound so easy. But it's not. I have never felt so completely uncoordinated in my life. I bet Abe could do a better job, and he's a dog. I'm like the tin girl who can't bend her arms and legs. All I can do is swivel on one foot.

Mom turns on some music. "Feel the beat, Ruby. Connect to the music, like when you play the piano."

I tilt my head to the side. "That's with my fingers, Mom. Not the same. Not at all."

But Mom isn't giving up yet. "Just step side to side to the rhythm. Like this."

Mom demonstrates. It's super embarrassing when your mom is a better dancer than you are.

I try to watch her feet and follow her back and forth and side to side. Then she throws me off by spinning around. Her hair whirls around her like a golden cape.

"Whoa, Mom. Way too much," I tell her.

"You can do it," she says. "Close your eyes for a minute. Imagine you are dancing along with the music. No one is going to watch you. Just dance what is in your heart."

I close my eyes. Listen to the rhythm of the music. And try to move along with it. I am a graceful butterfly, able to shift and glide with grace. My lavender wings are speckled with light blue like drips of paint. They flutter delicately. I float on the breeze, touching down on a rose, then lifting off again. Suddenly, I realize my wings are still wet with paint. Only it's too late. They stick together like glue. And I plummet to the ground, landing in a flower bush.

I look up to see Mom standing over me, offering me a hand. I'm not exactly in a flower bush. I'm in Abe's dog bed. Abe's dog bed is known for two things:

1. No one except Abe ever sits in it because, duh, it's a dog bed.
2. It is so covered with layers of Abe's fur that you can't tell what color it is anymore.

"Let's try again," Mom says with a grin as she pulls me to my feet. Only she doesn't let go of my hands, and we dance around the room together. Fur flies off my shirt to float in the air. (It sounds prettier than it looks.)

"This is actually kind of fun!" I call out.

Mom laughs. "It's supposed to be fun!"

We dance around and around the room until the song ends. And then we fall onto the sofa. We lie there side by side.

Mom brushes my hair back off my face. "Ruby, I think you're wrong. You can dance. You can do anything you want to do—as long as you believe in yourself."

I sit up and look at her. "That's the trouble. Sometimes I don't believe in myself." Like when my book club disappears to the other side of the playground. And my best friend partners up with the new girl for a class project.

"Everyone has moments like that. Even when they're grown up. I sometimes have those moments at work. Even now. But you know what I do? I remind myself who I am. And I think of something I like about myself." She hugs me close. "Maybe you could try that next time."

"Maybe" is my answer. Maybe I could also discover I am secretly a superhero. And tomorrow, instead of going to school, I could save the world from destruction. My superpower would be a magical pickle wand that would make people do anything I told them to do. I think I'd look pretty good in a bright-green cape zooming around on fire-powered roller skates.

CHAPTER 5

Trouble with a Lowercase *t*

The next morning, I have butterflies in my stomach. Actually, they aren't butterflies; they are tennis balls bouncing around inside me. Butterflies are light and airy with fluttering wings that would tickle my stomach. What I feel is a pounding, like a furry, neon tennis ball is loose inside me.

The morning bell is about to ring when I run up the stairs with my backpack. Siri is already in line. So are Jessica and Daisy. Charlotte stands behind them. I remember Gram's words yesterday. *Maybe being here is hard for Charlotte. Maybe she just wants to make friends.* I can be her friend too. (This is what's called being optimistic. I'm an optimistic kind of girl.)

I line up behind Charlotte. She turns around and waves.

"Hi," I say with a big smile. She smiles back.

"Ready for your dance today?" I think for a tiny second that she is making fun of me. It's not what she says. It's how she says it. There's something in her voice that sounds a little teasing. It sounds like the question mark at the end of her question is turned sideways a little bit so it can laugh at me. But I know I have a big imagination, so I tell myself it's nothing. I nod.

"Super ready," I answer. I am ready. I have planned the whole thing out. And in front of my mirror, it was splendid. (It really was. Not like an oddball grandma or a tin girl at all.)

Charlotte turns back around. And that's when I see them.

Pink laces.

In Charlotte's sneakers.

She is wearing Unicorn laces.

The drool-covered tennis balls in my stomach hit me so hard I make a sound. Something like a whoosh comes out of my mouth.

Whooooooooooosh.

Charlotte turns to look at me, her eyebrows raised. She is waiting for me to explain the strange sound.

I shrug, clear my throat, and say the first thing that comes to my mind. "Hair ball." (Remember Number 3 about me—saying a lot of things without thinking? Well, this is a perfect example—telling Charlotte I am part cat, and the gross part too. The part that vomits up balls of hair from licking itself.)

I see myself suddenly morph into a creature. My face stretches into a cat face with whiskers and tawny fur. My body grows paws instead of hands and feet. My tail waves in the air. I am not a pet cat; I am a lion. I have giant teeth and a growl that can be heard from miles away. I am fearless and powerful. The first thing I do is chew the laces right out of Charlotte's shoes. Then I vomit them up in a giant lion hair ball.

★ ★ ★

I am still coughing when the bell rings. Charlotte has stepped a short distance away from me. I follow her pink laces into the classroom. As I hang up my backpack and pull out my homework folder, my mind is only thinking one thing: Who told Charlotte to wear pink laces? And why didn't anyone tell me? (Wait, that's two things. My mind is thinking two things at once, like one of those wishbones from a turkey. It starts out as one thought and splits into two. Maybe I'm some kind of incredible genius brainiac who can do things no one else can do, like a young Einstein in training.)

Today we have extra partner time to work on our Statue of Liberty projects. Yay, me. At least Will B doesn't smell like salami today.

By lunch, I have to force the smile onto my face. I can feel the muscles stretching and pulling back like they just don't want to curve up. But I force them into something like a smile. I think.

I eat my apple and pretzels without saying much. No one notices anyway. They are all surrounding wonderful Charlotte. My friends crowd next to her, sharing her gummy worms. Who brings gummy worms for lunch? Do they have any nutritional value? Is loading up on sugar in the middle of the school day a great idea?

Absolutely and completely

Not.

A.

Good.

Idea.

And the only person who would bring a lunch like that is someone trying to win friends. Note to self: never underestimate the power of the gummy worm.

Maybe I am cranky because they all seem to like Charlotte so much better than me. "We never chose a book for next week's meeting," I say softly.

No one notices. So I try again a bit louder. *"We need to choose a book for next week."*

Now, all four heads turn to look at me. There. Much better, I think.

"We didn't finish though," Jessica tells me, as if I can't remember the horror that was yesterday.

"Yeah, I thought we would just do *Black Beauty* again," Siri adds.

I shrug. "No one seemed that excited. I thought maybe we should try a new book."

Jessica shakes her head. "I like *Black Beauty*. It's a classic. And anyway, I finished it last night. I want to talk about the ending."

"I'm almost done," Daisy adds. "And I like it too."

Siri shrugs. "That's not why we left. It wasn't the book. We just wanted to try being in a play."

She might as well have told me that the

reason she left was because I was boring. And Charlotte was interesting. My stomach twinges, like I've swallowed a flamingo, and it is poking me with its long, curvy beak.

"Then I guess we'll stick with *Black Beauty* for next Tuesday." I give in. Charlotte gives me a small smile. I am not sure if it is meant to be a nice smile or an *I won* smile. I smile a teeny smile back (which could be a nice smile or a *game's on* smile).

After we finish eating, everyone wants to work on the play. Charlotte places us in our spots. I stand next to Siri.

"Princesses, show me your best dance. Then I will decide who may go to the ball," Charlotte says in a queenly voice.

The game seems a little babyish to me. I mean, I stopped playing princesses in kindergarten. We're fifth graders now. I think we could come up with something a little bit more grown-up than *Cinderella*.

I turn to Siri to say something about it, but then I see the look on her face. She is smiling at Charlotte like Charlotte is a movie star or something. So I keep my mouth closed, but I can't help a half eye roll. (A half eye roll usually can go completely unnoticed except to the eye roller who knows they are rolling their eyes.)

"I'll go first," Siri says. Siri can do a back handspring, pitches on an all-boys' (except for her) baseball team, and wants to be a fashion designer when she grows up. I have never known her to be a good dancer. Until now, that is. All I can do is stand there, watching. I realize my mouth is hanging open like that kid Jason who falls asleep in class every day and drools all over his books. So I close it quick before saliva drips onto my shoes.

Siri is spinning, leaping, even twirling with her leg like the ballerina inside a jewelry box Gram gave me when I turned six. She is even better than Charlotte.

Siri finishes with a deep curtsy. We all clap and holler for her. I scream the loudest. After all, she is my best friend. Before I can give her a high five, Charlotte runs to Siri and hugs her tight.

Then Charlotte turns to me. "Your turn." I think she might actually be smirking instead of smiling. I know it's hard to tell the difference between a smirk and a smile because they both curve the mouth upward the same way. But a smirk is bratty, while a smile is happy. And the look Charlotte gives me is definitely of the bratty type.

I try to remember Mom's advice. *Think of something I like about myself.* All I can think about is how lame my dance will look. Mine is the dance version of a paint-by-the-numbers picture. It's a dance-by-the-numbers routine.

Jessica calls out, "Go, Ruby!" And Daisy claps for me. I remind myself that the thing I like best about myself is my imagination. So I use it.

I am a princess locked in a witch's castle and guarded by a giant ogre with garlic breath. I think I can slip out of the dungeon and slide down the castle wall on my magical hoverboard, but first I have to distract the ogre. So I dance around remembering to mouth-breathe while I spin in circles. My skirts whirl so fast they make the ogre dizzy. When he closes his eyes, I slide right through the window, activate my hoverboard, and fly to freedom.

I slide to a stop, arms outstretched to touch the air. Only I am standing before my friends. Correction: three friends and one sort-of friend. All of them are statues. They are staring at me, and no one is clapping or even smiling. I freeze, wondering if I have completely and totally humiliated myself. If I have ever wanted to be invisible, this is the moment. Then Jessica breaks the silence and grabs my arms.

"Ruby, you did it! You danced!"

Daisy joins her, giving me a high five. "You were like a real princess!"

Siri hugs me. "And you said you couldn't dance."

Even Charlotte manages to smile at me and says, "Good job."

I shrug. "Thanks." I try to act like it doesn't matter that much to me. But inside I am jumping up and down like it's Christmas morning. I did it. I really did it.

The good feeling stays with me all the way to the end of the day. Mrs. S has to help at the pickup line in front of school. Teachers trade off the job each week. The teachers hate when it's their turn, but the students love it because we get out of class ten minutes early.

"What are you wearing for Halloween?" Jessica asks Charlotte on the way down the steps. I watch as she bites into a mini chocolate-chip cookie from Charlotte.

Charlotte tilts her head to the side. Her ponytail bounces on the edge of her shoulder. She offers Siri a cookie next. "I don't know yet. I was thinking about being a pop star. You know, with a microphone and maybe a pink wig. What about you?"

Jessica grins, looking at Daisy before answering. "We're going as Thing 1 and Thing 2—from *The Cat in the Hat*. We love Dr. Seuss."

"I'm going as a butterfly," Siri says, cookie in hand.

"Did you make up your mind yet?" Daisy asks me. Somehow she has a cookie now too. I notice that everyone is eating the mini cookies. Everyone, that is, except me. Charlotte hasn't offered me one. I'm not hungry, but it's the point of it. If someone gives something to everyone else around you, but leaves you (and only you) out, it makes you really want that thing, even if you didn't want it in the first place. That's a really long way of saying *I want a cookie*!

"Any ideas?" Jessica adds.

I haven't decided what to be for Halloween. I always have a hard time choosing. Sometimes I don't decide until October 30. This is why Halloween is my mother's least favorite day of the year. She always has to scramble around to find a costume for me at the last minute. I'd like to be more considerate and make a decision early, but choosing between characters in my favorite books is like choosing only one chocolate from a candy shop. It's not an easy decision. It takes time.

I shake my head. "Not yet. I'm considering Dorothy, Hermione, or Alice."

Siri grins at me, then turns to Charlotte. "Ruby always dresses as a character from a book. So that's Dorothy from *The Wizard of Oz*, Hermione from Harry Potter, and Alice—"

"Let me guess. *In Wonderland*," Charlotte finishes for her with an eye roll.

"Do you have a problem with *Alice in Wonderland*?" I ask. My head tilts to the side, and I'm pretty sure I narrow my eyes too.

"Ruby!" Siri gives me a look. The kind of look that says you need to shut your mouth and not say another word. I see this look on my mother sometimes.

"Just asking," I say without looking away from Charlotte.

She shrugs. Closing the bag of cookies and

tossing them into the trash. Now I know for sure I am not getting that mini cookie. "Not really. It just seems kind of boring."

Boring? *Boring?* What could possibly be boring about *Alice in Wonderland*?

"What's boring about one of the greatest characters ever written? She's brave and smart and makes friends with all kinds of creatures without judging them." I could go on and on, but I stop there. I stop because Charlotte is judgy, while Alice is not.

Charlotte pretend yawns.

Now I know for absolute sure that I am narrowing my eyes. "Who asked you anyway?" It's not a great comeback, especially since I was the one who asked her. But I have to go with it for two reasons:

1. It's already out there.
2. I can't think of anything else.

"I'd rather live my life than read about someone else's life," Charlotte says with a smirk.

I'm not going to lie. Her words are like a slap to my face. My cheek burns pink as though she has actually touched it. I can feel all the eyes on me, waiting for me to do something. So I do.

"What's your problem with books, anyway? What did they ever do to you? Or haven't you ever read one?"

I wish I could take the words back. I wish I could rewind and handle this differently. It's not like me to lash out. And now I'm in big trouble. There are two kinds of trouble: trouble with a capital T and trouble with a lowercase t. Trouble with a capital T gets you sent to the principal. It's things like cheating or hitting someone or breaking something that doesn't belong to you. I don't get in that kind of trouble. Trouble with a lowercase t—now that's my specialty. Lowercase t trouble is something you wish you hadn't done, but it's too late to take it back. You can't fix it without calling more attention to the problem.

That's what I have done. I have started a war with Charlotte. And there is no going back.

We've reached the front of school. Charlotte walks away without another word. Then she looks over her shoulder at Siri. "Coming?" It doesn't come out like a question. It's more like a command you would give to a dog. I know this because Siri gives me a *sorry* look and then follows Charlotte to the pickup line. Daisy and Jessica haven't moved. They are still watching me, as if they are waiting to see what I will do next.

My nose starts to burn, and then my eyes get watery. I Am Not Going to Cry at School. Not now. Not ever. Not unless I trip while running the mile during PE because my shoelace has come untied, and I split my chin open and need twelve stitches. That's the only time I might need to cry, and then only if absolutely necessary.

"You can go ahead," I tell them in a quiet voice. "I'm going to wait here for my mom." I pull out a copy of *The Secret Garden*. I have always wanted to read this book, ever since my mom gave it to me. This is the exact copy of the book she read when she was my age. I hold it tightly in my hands, looking down at the drawing of the secret garden. And I wish I could escape into it, if only for the next ten minutes. Or maybe the rest of the year.

I hold a heavy golden key in my hand. The key opens the
door to a secret garden. I step through the door into a
magical world filled with flowers in every color. I sit down on
the path and breathe in the smell of roses and lilac. Nothing
bad can happen here. Birds sing. Bees buzz. And none of
them even try to sting me. Maybe I can stay here and live
in a burrow or a beehive. Bees probably don't have to go
to school. I bet their friends don't leave them at book club
either. Yellow and black aren't the worst of colors.

CHAPTER 6

Sorry Is Harder to Say than Spell

I don't eat much for dinner. No one really notices though. Wednesday night is Mom's book club, so we have a regular order with Charlie's Pizza. They deliver three pizzas at 6:00 p.m. Two are for us and one for book club.

I always sit in on Mom's meetings. I like to get ideas for my own book club. But not tonight. "I'm really tired," I tell Mom. (I throw in a fake yawn to emphasize the point.) She gives me a look with raised eyebrows that tells me she doesn't believe me. But she doesn't push. She's already asked me about school and my dance. "Fine" and "fine" were my answers. But my day was anything but *fine*.

Abe is the only one I can talk to. Even though he's a dog, Abe seems to understand when I am sad about something. He must have special canine powers. He jumps onto my bed and makes himself comfortable. I sit down next to him. He's almost as sweet as the bees in my imagination. And he's way smarter.

"I wouldn't have made you proud today," I whisper so softly that only he can hear. "I didn't make myself proud either. I kind of let myself down, Abe."

Abe looks up at me with his big brown eyes. I think he looks a little sad. "I didn't mean to say something awful. It just flew out of my mouth. And then I couldn't take it back. Everyone had already heard it. I bet they think I'm super mean. I guess I just didn't know what to do when Charlotte hurt me like that. So I copied her. And hurt her right back." Abe licks my hand. He makes it all wet, and he has the worst doggie breath in the world, but right now, I don't even care. I just let him slobber on me.

"You want me to say *sorry*, don't you?" I look down at him, and Abe wags his tail. "How can one word be so easy to write and so hard to say?" Abe doesn't have an answer for this one. "I think she should say *sorry* too. For ruining my book club and stealing my friends and insulting me." But I can tell Charlotte isn't the apologizing type. So I can't expect that. "Don't give an apology with an expectation of getting something in return," Mom always says. And she's right. *Sorry* doesn't mean much if you're only saying it to get something.

"Why is it that just when I get used to things, they have to go and change on me?" I wonder out loud. I was happy with my class and my friends and our routine. Then Charlotte had to come and turn everything upside down. For some reason, thinking of things turning upside down reminds me of *Alice in Wonderland*. She fell down a rabbit hole and even though she was far away from everything she knew, she still managed to make friends—and stay true to herself.

Dorothy did the same in *The Wizard of Oz*. And Hermione started out without even one friend—and ended up making two best friends without ever changing. I can be like them. I can stay true to myself and keep friends. I don't have to turn into Charlotte. I just have to be me. Ruby Josephine Starr. (Just try to guess where my middle name came from. I'll give you one hint: it's from a book.)

★ ★ ★

The next morning, I get to school right before the bell is about to ring (which I sort of planned. I might have to go to school, but I don't have to do the morning hello thing). Charlotte and Siri are already lining up. Jessica and Daisy are walking together. Siri sees me and gives a half wave.

Charlotte turns away to get her backpack. But I know she has seen me too. I go to the back of the line and stand next to Will P. Today, he is wearing socks with different-colored mustaches.

"Can't wait for the field trip," Will tells me.

The field trip is today. "I totally forgot," I admit. We're having a field trip, but we aren't actually leaving school. The field trip is coming to us. "They should have some other name for a field trip that isn't really a field trip because we don't go anywhere."

"I don't care what we call it. It's going to be amazingly fantastical," Will answers. He likes to put adjectives together, kind of like an adjective string. Sometimes he even makes up words. But you can understand what he means, so I guess it's OK.

"Totally," I say. But I am less than enthusiastic. Activities involve pairings. Pairings are just one more chance for me to be left out. (No one wants to be a single scoop of sour apple when everyone else is a double scoop of fun, like bubble gum or mint chip.)

Mrs. Sablinsky takes us into the classroom then. Siri says hi at the backpack rack. I smile back, but my smile is wobbly on the edges. Then Charlotte hands Siri a folded note before going to her desk. They smile at each other. All I can do is stare at the note, wishing I knew what it said.

I close my eyes and feel myself changing into another form. I
am a shape-shifter, and I can become anything I want. Today,
I become a golden hawk. My arms become wings, and my
skin turns into golden shimmery feathers. I fly over the classroom, soaring closer to Siri. I dip low enough for my talons to
snatch the note out of her hands. Then I fly away. Far away.
I leave the note at the top of the highest peak where only
the bravest warriors and hawks will ever find it.

Someone touches me. I see Daisy with her hand on my raised arm. I am still standing next to the backpacks.

"What are you doing?" Daisy asks, her dark eyes searching mine.

I drop my arms to my sides. "Just stretching," I tell her.

Mrs. Sablinsky begins to take roll so we hurry to our seats. I can't help but look across the room at Siri. She is reading the note. That's when I feel the pain in my chest, like someone is pinching me inside. Over and over again until I can barely breathe.

I know what it is. It's olive green and makes you kind of queasy.

Jealousy.

I swallow really hard, like if I gulp it down, it will go away. But there it is, pinching me again. It hurts.

★ ★ ★

Usually, math is the slowest part of the day. But not today. Today, it practically zooms by. Why is it that time seems to speed up when you want it to slow down? Are the minutes still sixty seconds long—or is there some secret time warp where they actually go faster but we can't really tell?

Before I know it, Mrs. S is telling us it's time for the field trip. I wish I had more division to do. Something must be seriously wrong with me.

Our class walks together to the multipurpose room. Somehow, I end up next to Charlotte.

"At my school, we actually left school for our field trips. I never heard of staying at school for one."

I don't know why everything Charlotte says makes me defensive. I don't even necessarily disagree with her about the idea of a field trip that isn't really a field trip. But I feel like I have to defend my school. Somehow, her words make it seem like she thinks our school is lame compared to her old one.

So I open my big mouth again. And I don't say *sorry*. No, instead, I make it even worse.

"Well, this is your school now, right? And this is how we do things here."

Ugh. Not how I meant it to come out at all. And now everyone is looking at me like they don't know me again. I wish I could climb right into the nearest trash can.

I know what I need to do. I just can't seem to do it. I try to say *sorry*, but nothing comes out. The word is stuck in my throat. I cough loudly. Making everyone stare at me even more. So I decide to wait for lunch to apologize.

The field trip that isn't really a field trip is all about... No, it can't be. But it is. It's about *friendship*.

We all sit in rows on the floor of the multi-purpose room facing the stage. I end up pushed to the end of the line so I'm not even sitting by any of the Unicorns. I'm actually sitting between Jason (the boy who sleeps all day) and Will B (yes, *that* Will). Everyone knows that one of the best parts of any field trip is being with your friends. Only I'm not with my friends. I'm not even with any sort-of friends.

Suddenly, I am distracted from my less-than-fantastic seating arrangement as the curtains open and six acrobats in matching shiny, red outfits run across the stage doing flips. Everyone starts oohing and aahing. Then one performer waits in the middle of the stage while a second performer runs and somersaults to stand on his shoulders. The next acrobat jumps even higher because he lands on the second one's shoulders. They keep going higher and higher until the last one runs and jumps on a little trampoline to reach the very tippy top.

The whole class jumps to their feet clapping and cheering. Even Mrs. Sablinsky has a smile on her face. I'm pretty sure it's a smile anyway.

One by one, the acrobats somersault down to stand in a line facing us. The lead performer picks up a microphone. "Hey, everybody. We're here to share our secret with you. Do you want to know how we just did that?" He doesn't wait for an answer. "Cooperation! We worked together. Each one of us helped the group to succeed. We trust each other. If we didn't, then one of us might fall. Watch this!"

They line themselves up sideways and make a bridge. Then one of the acrobats does seven back handsprings in a row. Right across the bridge!

"Now it's your turn," the main acrobat tells us. He raises his hands to tell us to stand up.

I think he means we are going to learn tumbling. I've always wanted to be like the gymnastics girls in the Olympics. This might be the best field trip that isn't really a field trip ever!

I scramble to my feet along with everyone else. Even Jason wakes up for this. Only, it's not what I think. Not at all.

The lead performer tells us to pair up. This can't be happening to me again. I look around quickly to see if I can spot any of the Unicorns. Jessica and Daisy are in the row ahead of me. I can't see Siri at all. My eyes dart around, looking for someone who is alone. Any second now, Mrs. S is going to ask the dreaded question, "Who still needs a partner?" That's when I see Molly. She usually pairs with Hazel, but she's standing alone. I hurry over.

"Wannabepartners?" I ask as quickly as I can.

"Sure," she answers with a small smile.

The acrobats begin passing out balloons while the one on the microphone explains the exercise. "Sit down back to back with the balloon in between. Then work together to stand up, while keeping the balloon between you."

This is way more difficult than it sounds. Molly and I get a yellow balloon. We put it between our backs and try to stand. Only every time one of us moves, the balloon drifts away. We have to run and catch it and start the whole thing over.

The second time it happens, the balloon drifts to the back of the room. I chase it down only to find myself looking right at Siri and Charlotte. Except they don't see me. Because the two of them are standing up with the balloon perfectly balanced between their backs. They look like they should be teaching the class.

Which is exactly what the acrobat says a few minutes later. He invites Charlotte and Siri up onstage.

"You two kept the balloon in place the longest, so you get to demonstrate the hardest of all trust exercises—the trust fall."

The rest of us are asked to sit down again. We won't be trying this one at all.

I sit down next to Molly and watch as Siri is asked to close her eyes and fall backward, trusting that Charlotte will catch her. The other acrobats stand nearby in case Charlotte misses.

Only she doesn't. Siri falls backward, and Charlotte catches her.

"And that's trust, everybody!" the acrobat calls out. "Let's give them a big round of applause."

Then he hands them each a special sticker and shakes their hands. "Keep up the good friendship."

There's only so much a girl can take. I think it should be me up there with Siri.

I imagine my friends are wearing matching shiny pink outfits
and are onstage. Jessica is standing on Mrs. Sablinsky's
shoulders. Daisy is standing on Jessica's shoulders. And Siri
is standing on Daisy's shoulders. I run onstage and leap onto
the trampoline. When I bounce into the air, Siri is supposed
to catch my hands. But she misses. Charlotte is jumping from
the other side. Siri reaches for Charlotte's hands instead of
mine. I fall to the ground, which is actually a giant bowl of
cherry Jell-O.

The six acrobats run across the stage doing flips while we leave the auditorium. The lunch bell is about to ring. I know what I need to do.

CHAPTER 7

Unicorns Rule

We walk to the lunch benches and squeeze in. I make sure to sit next to Charlotte. I think maybe if I whisper the word before my brain realizes what I am going to say, that will work better. It doesn't. I end up choking on a tortilla chip. It's so bad that Daisy jumps up and runs over to clap me on the back.

"You OK?" Siri asks.

I just nod. I feel like one of those rocks that has googly eyes glued on it. Completely ridiculous. (I mean why does a rock want to have a face anyway? It's a rock. It's all natural and part of the earth and everything. Why does it want to look like a wannabe stuffed animal?)

But that's what I am. A pet rock.

I see myself sitting at the table with my friends. Only I am not me. I am an oval-shaped grayish rock with two googly eyes. I am even wearing a pink sweater. Everyone gets up from the table and leaves. I have to stay right where I am because, of course, I am a rock. I am not on the ground with the other rocks, the rocks that don't have googly eyes. I am completely and totally alone.

I am the first one to get up from the table. I do not want to be left behind. My friends follow me to the four square courts. And there I grimace my way through the wonderful world of Charlotte's play game.

"I liked both of your dances. But only one of you can go to the ball. Close your eyes. If I tap you on the shoulder, you are going to the ball."

This game gets worse by the minute.

But I close my eyes. Because Siri is closing hers. Of course, there is no tap on my shoulder. So when I hear Charlotte say, "You can open your eyes now," I'm not surprised to see Siri jumping up and down.

"I'm going to the ball!"

I have to spend the rest of lunch watching everyone else dance around at a ball. I just sit on the blacktop by myself.

But when the bell rings, I walk right up to Charlotte. Maybe all that time being bored was good for something. Now I am ready.

"Can I talk to you for a minute?" I say.

She looks at Siri before answering me. "Sure."

I step to the side, and Charlotte steps with me. My friends move toward the class line. I know they are trying not to eavesdrop.

"I just wanted to say *sorry*." There. I did it. "I know you just got here, and it must be hard for you. I didn't mean to say the things I said."

Charlotte smiles at me. I can see her pink braces and everything. "Thanks, Ruby. I really want to be your friend."

"Me too," I answer.

By then we have reached the class line. Charlotte moves behind Jessica. I stand behind Charlotte. I smile to myself.

I think that is the end of it. That everything will be all right after this little talk. It will be just like it was before Charlotte, only with Charlotte. The Unicorns will be as strong and powerful as ever.

★ ★ ★

PE is at the end of the school day. Today, we have to run the mile. Siri and I usually pair up so we can talk while we jog. Still, with everything that's been happening lately, I wouldn't be surprised if she sticks with Charlotte. Except she doesn't. She comes over to run with me.

"Did you like the field trip?" I ask her.

Siri grins. "I thought it was amazing. Especially the way they could flip in the air."

"Even Mrs. Sablinsky liked it," I add.

"Charlotte thought the whole thing was lame," Siri shares. "Because we didn't leave school. She wasn't even happy we got to go onstage."

I shrug. I'm not sure I want to talk about Charlotte. I might get all angry and say something I have to apologize for again. Saying *sorry* more than one time in a day is just too much.

"You like her, right?" Siri mentions Charlotte,

not me. I keep my eyes forward on the ground in front of me, and not on Siri. "I mean, you haven't really been yourself the last few days. Saying things and stuff."

(Important fact about best friends: sometimes they tell you something you really don't want to hear, even though you know it's the truth.)

I shrug again. "I don't know. She's kind of making things different. I said *sorry*, you know." I don't know why I feel like I need to tell her. But somehow, I do. I want her to know I apologized for the things I said. Even if I didn't have to apologize to Charlotte.

Siri smiles. "Different can be good. It's interesting." She doesn't mention the apology part. Maybe because there isn't anything to say about it.

"I guess. But what about book club?" I ask her. There, I've said it.

"What about book club?" Siri and I round the yard for the second lap.

How do I explain all the things I am thinking without sounding jealous? I decide to keep it simple. Stick to the facts. "I mean she didn't even read the book."

Siri's mouth tightens. I can tell she is going to defend Charlotte before she even says the words. "Maybe she didn't have time. It was her first day."

"I guess." This must be my new standard phrase. *I guess.* (It's kind of like shrugging without the shrug.)

What I want to say is that Siri shouldn't have invited Charlotte into the Unicorns without asking me first. And that only people who love books should be part of the Unicorns. Book club isn't a theater club. It's for reading.

"I'm sure next Tuesday will be just like always." Siri gives me her pink-braces grin. And I can't help but smile back.

"Let's race," I say. We run our fastest around

the yard, side by side. I stretch my legs out and ignore the cramp in my side. I just run.

★ ★ ★

Mom makes tortilla soup and quesadillas for dinner. There are options without meat, with meat, and gluten-free. Every choice looks delicious to me. My stomach makes a little rumbling sound to remind me I didn't eat much at lunch today.

"Sunday, we're going over to Grandma and Grandpa's," Mom tells us. She passes around a platter of chips and salsa.

I dip a triangle of quesadilla into sour cream. Secret factoid about me: I love, absolutely *love*, sour cream. It's the best part about quesadilla night. "For Grandpa's birthday," I pipe in with my mouth full.

"And decorating," Connor adds. It's a family tradition. Every year, we help our grandparents decorate their front yard for Halloween. They live on a cul-de-sac so their house is super popular on

Halloween. The street is blocked off, and all the homes are decorated like it's a street party.

"Your grandfather has asked for only handmade gifts," Dad adds as he bites into a chip. It makes a crunchy sound. *Crunch. Crunch. Crunch.* Dad chews really loud.

"Not like this is a news flash. He says the same thing every year," Sam comments.

"So true." Mom speaks up. "But it's more meaningful to receive gifts from the heart."

I am digging into my tortilla soup when I proudly announce, "I already know what I am giving Grandpa."

Everyone waits for me to answer. They know I like to make announcements in two parts. The first part is the introduction. I wait a beat for the suspense to kick in. And then I hit them with the second part—the content. In this case, what I am actually giving Grandpa.

"A poem. About George and Abe."

"*Très magnifique*," Dad responds.

"I thought I'd bake a cake, if anyone wants to help," Mom offers.

"I'll help!" "Me too!" Sam and I speak at the same time. Sam loves sports and all, but his secret favorite hobby is cooking. We watch cooking shows together all the time. He wants to be a chef when he grows up.

Connor, on the other hand, doesn't want to be anywhere near the kitchen, unless he's performing a scientific experiment.

I see myself in the kitchen mixing cake ingredients in a giant bowl. I add vanilla, butter, flour, and eggs. Next to me, Connor has his own mixing bowl. He is adding grass, leaves, dead ants, and dirt. I lean over my bowl and sniff the sweet smell. Connor leans over his bowl and breathes in. I roll my eyes. Connor switches bowls when I am not looking. I bake dead ants and dirt into a cake for Gramps.

After that, we all share stories about our days. I don't tell them about Charlotte and the Great Apology. Some things are just too personal to share at the dinner table. Instead, I wait until bedtime. Mom sits on my bed, and we read a little together from *The Secret Garden*. We take turns reading pages until we finish a chapter.

"I like Mary," Mom says. "She has spunk. Kind of like you. She isn't afraid to follow her heart."

"Sometimes she says things she shouldn't though," I say. "I do that too."

"Like with your friends?" Mom asks, putting the book down and looking at me. She brushes a curl back from my cheek. It is still damp from my shower.

I shrug. "Sometimes I say things I wish I hadn't said. Only it's too late to call them back. And then sometimes I say another something that makes it even worse."

"We all do that, Ruby. It takes wisdom to

know when to speak and when to stay silent. Time will help. And experience." Mom touches her finger to the tip of my nose. She has done that since I was really little. She told me once it used to make me laugh. Now it just makes me feel like a grilled cheese—all gooey and melty.

I put my arms around Mom and hold her tight. As if holding her this tight can make me shrink back to being four or five even. I'd like to go back to some earlier age when things were easier. Then I hear her voice above me. Her chin is resting on the crown of my head, right where my princess tiara would be (if I had one).

"Why don't you invite Siri over this weekend? Or Jessica or Daisy."

I shake my head. I don't say the words though. I don't think they can come out without tears. But the truth is, I can't take the rejection. If I ask one of them to come over and they say no, it will crush me.

I don't tell Mom. I think she probably under-stands this anyway. Because she says, "How about spending some time with me, instead?"

I nod my head this time. I'm sure things will get better at school. I just need the space of a weekend to figure things out. After that, I'm sure everything will be back to normal.

CHAPTER 8

The Freakiest Friday Ever

Friday mornings, our whole school meets in the auditorium. We have an assembly with announcements about events, and sometimes we do something fun, like get prizes or win tickets for Popsicles at lunch. Today, when I get to school, Siri already has a seat for me at the end of the row.

She waves to me and points to the seat next to her. "For you."

"Thank you. And a good morning to you," I answer using my fake British accent. (Secret factoid about me: I like to speak with a British accent whenever possible. It makes me sound smarter, and also like I belong at Hogwarts.)

As I slip into the seat, I notice Charlotte sitting on the other side of Siri.

"I've been telling Charlotte about what happens at Friday assemblies," Siri says, flipping her braids back and forth as she looks from me to Charlotte and back again. I have two thoughts:

1. I wonder if Siri is going to pull a muscle in her neck?
2. Can this only be Charlotte's first Friday? (It seems like she has been here for months already.)

"The best part is when they hand out the weekly class prize," I tell Charlotte still in my British voice. After all, I am trying to be her friend now.

"Yeah, every week the class with the most spirit points gets to keep the trophy for a whole week!" Siri pipes in.

"Don't forget the extra recess and Popsicle party," I add.

"A Popsicle party sounds fun." Charlotte turns her shiny grin to me. "I hope our class wins!"

Then she looks at Siri. "How do you get spirit points?"

"Wearing school colors on Friday—that's red and white. Recycling our lunches. And participating in school events, like the spelling bee."

"I didn't know about the school colors," Charlotte says softly. She is wearing a yellow T-shirt with jeans.

I have on a red-and-white-striped T-shirt and a red sweatshirt. I pull off my sweatshirt and hand it over to Charlotte. "Here, you can borrow mine."

"Are you sure?" she asks.

I shrug. "You can give it back to me at the end of the day. I have a red-and-white shirt on too."

Siri squeezes my hand. "That's really nice of you, Ruby."

"We want points, don't we?" I say lightly. I act like sharing my favorite sweatshirt is no big deal. But it is a big deal. And I know that I am really trying to be Charlotte's friend. I am trying to think about how I would feel in her position. I would like someone to do the same for me.

"We might not win anyway," Siri says. "Mr. Penley's class has won for the last three weeks in a row."

"That's not fair," Charlotte says. "They should only let a class win once until everyone has had a chance."

I laugh. "You wouldn't be saying that if our class had won three times in a row and we were having Popsicles again today."

Charlotte laughs. "So true."

Then the bell rings, and our principal, Mr. Snyder, leads us in the flag salute. The assembly is short today. A few students make announcements about after-school activities and the upcoming book fair.

I am sitting in an auditorium full of book writers. All of us are holding the books we have written. Mine has a unicorn on the cover. I clutch it in my hands. My name is called out, and I stand, bowing to the applause, and make my way to the podium. There, I am presented with a trophy for writing the best book of the century. "Thank you," I say in a confident but humble voice. "I am honored to receive this award. My writing career began in the fifth grade." I am about to say more, but someone calls my name.

"Ruby! It's time!" I blink, remembering where I am.

"Finally!" I say to Siri. I scoot to the edge of my seat. Siri and I cross our fingers, and I close my eyes really tight.

"Mrs. Sablinsky's class in Room 15!"

"We won! We actually won!" I open my eyes and jump to my feet at the same time as Mrs. Sablinsky walks to the front of the auditorium. I have to say I do notice a little spring in her step. Even her frown looks a bit happier than usual.

I turn around to see Will P standing in the row behind me. "It's all that trash you picked up!"

Will P pats himself on the shoulder. "I am responsible," he agrees. "I am supremely eco-friendly."

Today, Will is wearing school spirit socks with red-and-white checks. I point to them. "Good choice," I tell him before turning back around to watch my teacher carry the trophy down the aisle.

The assembly ends after that, and we follow Mrs. Sablinsky back to class. She displays the trophy on her desk where we can all see it.

Journal writing zooms by, as always. I write all about Gramps and the Halloween decorating party we will have this weekend. Before I know it, Mrs. Sablinsky is giving us the spelling test. We have to print each word and then, next to it, write it in cursive as well. My cursive is pretty good, except for my *r*'s. They always come out looking like upside-down swings. I studied last night, and I am confident about the words. So I only really have to worry about those swingy *r*'s.

I write the words down as soon as Mrs. Sablinsky says them. I don't wait for her to use them in sentences. I want to have as much time as possible to make my cursive look fancy. The only word that kind of messes me up is *believe*. I can't remember if it is spelled like this:

believe

or

beleive

I decide to go for the *i* before the *e*. It looks better that way so I think it must be right. (Probably I have seen it that way on my study sheet.)

We roll right into the math test. Mrs. Sablinsky doesn't think we need breaks between exams. She's all about getting the hard stuff out of the way first thing.

The math test is easy-peasy, lemon-squeezy.

I finish really fast, but then I go back and check all my answers. After I turn in my test, I even have time to work on a word search. Mrs. S gives them out if we have extra time. I choose one in an upside-down magician's hat. It has all kinds of words having to do with magic. Like *disappear* and *illusion*. I even find *believe*. And guess what? It's spelled with the *i* before the *e*! So I got that one right!

```
s  p  e  c  t  a  c  u  l  a  r  d
w  m  b  y  d  q  k  m  a  g  i  c
t  e  r  a  b  b  i  t  m  p  z  y
i  l  l  u  s  i  o  n  m  n  r  o
e  p  e  r  f  o  r  m  e  r  c  q
a  b  d  r  e  a  l  i  t  y  m  v
u  i  o  y  m  k  w  p  a  x  l  d
v  a  u  d  i  e  n  c  e  d  k  g
l  p  b  e  l  i  e  v  e  m  x  b
n  f  s  d  i  s  a  p  p  e  a  r
r  e  a  p  p  e  a  r  a  n  c  e
h  g  k  v  w  d  p  n  t  e  m  s
c  u  o  a  p  p  l  a  u  s  e  j
```

The bell rings, and I hurry to my backpack for my lunch. All this testing has made me super-duper hungry. It must be my lucky day because Mom didn't give me my usual. Instead, I have a blueberry muffin and strawberries. I can't wait to eat them!

I spot Siri already walking through the door, so I hurry to catch up. But I get squished between two boys, and I lose track of her. I reach her at the lunch tables. She's already sitting with Charlotte. It kind of hurts that she didn't wait for me. Sort of like I just put my hand on a red ant and it stung me, but only for a second—almost not even long enough to realize. (Almost.)

I find a spot next to Jessica and open my lunch. I'm just about to bite into the blueberry muffin when this happens:

"Can't wait for tonight!" Charlotte says to Siri.

"Me either," Siri answers with a quick glance at me.

I'm afraid to ask. I know I shouldn't ask. But I just can't help myself, and the words come out anyway. "What's tonight?"

Glances go back and forth between Siri and Charlotte. Siri shrugs as though she is saying, *I might as well tell her.*

And then I know for real absolute sure that I shouldn't have asked.

"Charlotte is sleeping over tonight."

Oh.

Well.

A sleepover.

I don't even taste the blueberry muffin. It might as well be Abe's dog food. I consider skipping the strawberries altogether because I really have no appetite anymore. But Mom made this nice food for me, and the least I can do is eat it. So I eat the strawberries. They taste like sunshine and happiness. I think Mom sent them on purpose. Because somehow, she just made this day a little better.

And it's almost like she is here with me right now, telling me to look on the bright side.

Siri and I have other friends—of course we do. And we have other playdates even. (Now that we're in fifth grade, it seems kind of babyish to call them playdates though.) It's just that we don't have

Sleepovers.

Sleepovers are a best-friend kind of thing. Everyone knows that—everyone between the ages of eight and eighteen anyway. You don't stay up all night sharing secrets with someone you barely know. That's best-friend territory.

But obviously Siri doesn't know that.

I look over at her across the table. She didn't even sit next to me. She's sitting across the table next to Charlotte. Sharing a fruit leather with her.

Or maybe, the voice in my head says softly, maybe she *does* know that. And Charlotte is her new BFF. I hate that voice. It's like my own personal frenemy, always saying the things I'm afraid of saying.

I eat another strawberry for strength and ignore the voice. If we're all going to be friends, then let's get on with it. I plaster a giant smile on my face.

"Ready to play?"

Jessica wrinkles her eyebrows. "I thought you didn't like the princess game?"

I shrug. "It's growing on me, I guess."

"Great!" Charlotte answers, jumping to her hot-pink-laced feet.

★ ★ ★

Twenty minutes later, I am princessed out. So much that I am happy to return to class. As we line up, I notice that my sneaker has come untied. I lean down and quickly tie the hot-pink laces. But not before I notice Charlotte and Siri's feet side by side. I can see two pairs of matching laces. And for some reason, seeing the four hot-pink bows lined up like that unties my insides and makes my eyes a little watery. I duck my head and wipe the back of my hand across my eyes. Then I brush some loose curls off my face, drying my hand on my hair.

I'm not sure why the laces are my undoing—but they are. It takes all my strength and determination not to look again.

But I don't.

I won't.

I am in a dark cave, backed against a wall. An evil sorceress is holding me there with her dark power. She wants me to give her the one thing that will make her live forever. My imagination. I'm afraid if I give it to her, I will no longer see the impossible. Just then, a giant white tail sweeps the sorceress aside. It is my white dragon. "Queen Ruby," it calls out. I climb up onto the dragon's neck and hold on tight. The dragon flies high over the rainbow. I am free, and I am still me. Anything is possible.

CHAPTER 9

The Freakiest Friday Ever, Part 2!

Library is my absolute and total favorite classroom activity. The librarian is this really supernice lady named Mrs. Xia. She always talks to me about the classics. Book people kind of have this secret code language, like we're connected as part of a club or something. We recognize the same love of books in the other person's reaction to a simple question like, "What are you reading right now?"

When a book person answers that question, their eyes start to glow a little. You can see it in my mom, Mrs. Xia, Connor, and Jessica.

So today, when I see Mrs. Xia, she asks me right away. "What are you reading this week, Ruby?"

"*The Secret Garden*," I say with pride.

Mrs. Xia claps her hands together, and a wide smile spreads across her face like sunshine. "One of my favorites!"

And there it is, the book-people secret code.

Behind me, students are moving around the room, looking at the books. Mrs. Xia has set out Halloween titles for people to browse. But I already know exactly what I want.

"I'd like to find a cookbook today," I tell her. "I'm baking a cake for my grandfather's birthday this weekend. I could use some tips."

"Ah, we have some wonderful cookbooks. Over here." Mrs. Xia leads me to the nonfiction section of the library. On the shelf are cookbooks for every type of food—Italian, Mexican, Chinese, all-American favorites, French, Spanish. My mouth waters just looking at the titles. The next section is for baking. There are some fun books called *Princess Baking* and *Cupcake World* that I definitely want to check out another time. There is even a book on making candy. I think this could be a good choice too. But I am on a mission. So I select a book called *100 Cakes*. With a hundred cakes, I have to find at least one Grandpa would like!

I take my book to the front. My friends are standing in line already with their choices. Some people make library social time and choose books with their friends. Sometimes I do that too. Sometimes Siri and I even look for books that had doubles so we could get the exact same book. But not today. Today, I needed some air.

"Ruby, what are you getting?" Jessica asks.

"It's called *100 Cakes*. I'm baking a cake this weekend," I tell her as I flip the book around so she can see the cover. It shows a shiny chocolate cake with raspberries around the edges. The cover is seriously mouthwatering.

Jessica's eyes go wide. "That looks so good! Now I want some cake!"

"Me too!" Daisy says. "Are you going to make that one?"

I shrug. "I don't know. There are a hundred choices. Plus, Sam is helping me. I think we should choose together."

Siri speaks up then. "What are you making the cake for?"

"My grandfather's birthday on Sunday." Last year, she came with me to decorate. I try not to think about it.

"We had fun last year on his birthday," Siri reminds me. "Remember the pumpkin lights?"

I laugh, even though I am not in a laughing mood. I want to stay mad. "How could I forget my dad being stuck in a tree?"

We were helping Dad hang strings of light-up pumpkins in the trees in Gram's front yard. Dad thought it would be easier if he climbed into the tree instead of standing on a ladder. So he climbed up. He hung up the lights, and they looked great.

But then he realized his shirt was caught on a branch. He couldn't get it loose, and he couldn't pull his arms up to take it off. We had to wait for the fire department to come and get him out of the tree. Dad calls it his most embarrassing moment ever. Siri and I couldn't stop laughing for a whole week.

"I remember that!" Daisy says. And Jessica starts to giggle. We told our friends about it first thing the next day. So it was almost like they were there with us.

The only one who doesn't know about it is Charlotte. I catch the look on her face. And I realize that right now, she feels the same way I have felt since she got here—left out. Even though I should be happy that she is left out for once, I don't. I actually know what this feels like. I don't want someone else to experience it, not because of me anyway. So I tell her the story. I watch her face go from sad to happy, just like that.

"I wish I had a big family like yours," Charlotte says. "It's just me and my dad. And my grandma."

I want to ask her about her mom. It's a natural question after hearing it's just her and her dad and grandma. But just as I open my mouth to ask, I hear Mom's voice in my head. It's so loud it's almost like she is standing right next to me. *If Charlotte wants to tell you about her mother, she will. No need to pry.*

I close my mouth tight, pressing my lips into a thin line.

But Jessica doesn't have that voice in her head, or if she does, she doesn't listen to it. "What about your mom?"

I shoot Jessica a quick look, but it's too late because the words are already out there.

I watch Charlotte to see how she will react. I see sadness flicker in her eyes. Then she shrugs and looks down at her hands. "She left a long time ago."

There is a silent moment among us. Not one of us is without a mother. I look at Siri, who looks at Jessica, and Jessica looks at Daisy. Siri is the only one of the four of us who doesn't have both parents in the same house. Her parents are divorced, but she goes back and forth between them.

Charlotte bends down and pretends to tie her shoe. But I know it's just a cover. I know this because I have done it myself when I can't think of anything else to do.

"I'm sorry, Charlotte. That must be really hard for you." The words are out of my mouth before I even realize what I am saying.

Charlotte looks up at me. Her eyes are shiny. I know if she looks down, the tears will overflow. But right now, they are caught in her lashes. She shrugs. "No big deal. I don't remember her anyway."

"Everyone, please gather your books now. It's time to head back to the classroom." Mrs. Xia's voice interrupts us. I move behind Siri to line up at the door. Charlotte steps behind me. I sneak one look at her. But she doesn't notice. She is looking down at the ground. And I can't be positive, but I think I see one single silent tear slip off her cheek and drop onto the ground.

I imagine catching Charlotte's tear in my hand. The tear stays perfectly formed. It glistens with sorrow. I hold it gently in my hand. I am no longer in the library. I am in an empty white room with three doors. There is a red door, a blue door, and a green door. I open the blue door. Outside is an ocean of tears. All the sadness in the world is in that ocean. I slip the tear into the sea—and close the door.

When we get back to the classroom, we have silent reading time. I look through half of the one hundred recipes, using slips of paper to mark my favorites: a red velvet cake, a carrot cake with raisins, and the chocolate one from the cover. I don't have time to finish though, because I have to go outside. Every Friday, I help with the first, second, and third graders.

I am a yard guard. We're a group of fourth and fifth graders who help the younger students learn to play fair on the playground. We even get to wear red-and-white badges on red strings around our necks. Mrs. Sablinsky excuses me and Siri and the other yard guards. Siri and I hurry to the drawer in the back of the classroom for our badges. Then we head for the stairs.

"Did you find any good recipes?" Siri asks.

"I found a couple I liked. I wanted to find one with coconut though. I know Gramps loves it."

"Mmm, coconut frosting sounds really good right now," she says. "Your mom is the best baker."

"I know," I agree. Thinking about my mom baking reminds me that Charlotte doesn't have a mom.

"I felt really bad about Charlotte," I tell Siri.

"Her grandma picks her up every day, but your grandma picks you up when your mom is working too."

I guess that's true. But it's different for Charlotte.

The object of the yard guards is to look for kids that are having problems getting along. Maybe someone doesn't think they should be out in four square. Or maybe someone else cuts in line for the drinking fountain. Maybe someone just gets their feelings hurt. Yard guards are supposed to step in and help them work it out.

Siri and I join a really big game of basketball. I play on one team while Siri plays on the other team. Siri can make shots from the opposite side of the court. Me, I'm better at dribbling the ball than actually shooting it. So I hang toward the outside and feed the ball to the other players. When two boys begin to argue over whether someone is traveling, Siri and I step into the middle of the argument.

"Let's help figure this out," I suggest.

"Good idea," Siri agrees. "If someone isn't sure they traveled, give them another chance." She turns to the boy who has the ball. "Just remember, if your feet are moving, the ball has to be moving too."

"Got it," the boy answers. His hair dips over one eye, and he shakes it with a quick tilt of his head before bouncing the ball and shuffling toward the basket.

He misses, and the other team gets the ball. We all move to the other side of the court. There aren't any other arguments for Siri and I to work out with this group. So we move on and begin walking the perimeter of the playground. We keep our eyes open for yelling or crying. Everyone seems to be playing fair.

"I hope you don't feel weird," Siri says.

I think I'm pretty sure I know what she's talking about. But I don't want to say it if I am wrong. So I say this instead: "About what?"

Siri shrugs. She is playing with the yard guard badge around her neck. Twisting and untwisting the cord that holds the badge. I watch it spin instead of looking directly at her.

"You know, Charlotte coming over and all."

"Oh that." Somehow, the sleepover doesn't matter as much now. So I really mean it when I shrug and say, "No biggie."

"Her grandma called and asked me to stay at her house first," Siri explains. "But because I'm with my mom this weekend, it made more sense for her to come to my house." Siri spins the badge again. I want to reach out and stop it from spinning. But I don't.

"I get it," I say. I do. So then why does it make me feel so squirmy inside? I wish it didn't. But sometimes wishes don't come true. Sometimes things are just hard. And wishing doesn't make them any easier.

Siri exhales like she has been holding her breath or something. "Good, 'cause I didn't want you to think it was her being my best friend or anything. 'Cause you're my best friend."

I crack my face into a smile. Siri is my best friend. And I am her best friend. Charlotte is just spending the night. It really is no big deal.

Siri and I stand on the balcony of a silver castle. We wear matching crowns of woven purple and pink flowers. Below us are trees with golden blossoms, streams decorated with jewels, and fairies with butterfly wings floating in the air. This is the kingdom of friendship where we welcome everyone as our friend. Our motto is happiness.

CHAPTER 10

Pumpkins, Frosting, and a Pair of Dogs Do Not Mix

Saturday afternoon, Mom finds me and Abe snuggled on the sofa reading. Well, I'm reading. Abe is lying there with one eye open and one eye closed. "It's time to make Grandpa's birthday cake," Mom says. I look up at her. She is wearing her colorful, floral not-working clothes, and her hair is pulled into a ponytail.

"Let's go, Abe," I say as I follow Mom, and Abe follows me into the kitchen like a train. Mom is the engine, I am the middle, and Abe is the caboose. I like the word *caboose*. Just thinking of it makes me want to laugh.

Sam is sitting on the kitchen counter, leafing through my *100 Cakes* book.

"I like the ones you marked," he tells me. "Especially the red velvet. It looks so good in the picture."

I agree with him that cake does look super delicious. But I was thinking about something else. "I was hoping to find one with coconut since I know Grandpa loves it."

"And I just so happen to have this..." Mom reaches into the cabinet and holds up a pinkish-tan bag. "Coconut flakes."

Sam hands me the book. I flip to the back and look through the index to find...*C* for *coconut*. And there it is—coconut cake, page 56.

I turn to page 56 to see a white, fluffy angelic-looking cake that is exactly what I wanted to find.

I hold the book up so Sam and Mom can see it. "What do you think?" I ask.

My mom and brother look at each other and nod. "We like it," Mom says. Abe barks, and I laugh before I can catch myself. "I guess Abe likes it too," I tell them.

Mom heads to the pantry for the dry ingredients, and I take out butter and eggs. Sam sets up the mixing bowls and measuring cups. Mom flips on the old radio in the kitchen corner. It's the same radio Grandma used to have in their kitchen when my mom was growing up. It's already set to the oldies station. But Sam and I know all the words to the songs. Mom always sings while she cooks. We sing with her.

Sam cracks the eggs using only one hand. "It's all in the flick of the wrist," he tells me. "Want to give it a try?" I shake my head no. I have a feeling if I tried, I'd end up with more egg on the counter than in the bowl.

"I'll stick with flour and sugar," I say as I measure them one at a time. I use a butter knife to level the measuring cup. Mom says with baking, you need to follow the directions exactly.

When the batter is ready, I lean over the bowl and breathe deeply. It smells delicious. Then Sam pours it into the two round pans, and Mom slips them into the oven.

"We can take a little break while the cake is baking," Mom tells us. "How about a snack?"

I wasn't hungry earlier, but now I am starving. "Can I have an apple with peanut butter?" I ask Mom.

"Me too," Sam echoes.

"That makes three of us," Mom answers as she pulls out plates and spoons.

"Four," Connor says as he comes into the kitchen. It's a Starr family tradition. We all love peanut butter on spoons.

We sit together at the kitchen table and talk about books. If I'm not reading, talking about books is the next best thing. We all share a little about the books we are each reading right now. Connor is reading a book about snails. I think snails are slimy and gross when they get smushed and turn into brownish goo, but Connor shares some interesting facts. Here's one: Snails can live ten to fifteen years in captivity. Some have even lived twenty-five years.

Snails and cake don't really go together. But that's life with Connor. Pretty soon, the kitchen fills with the sweet scent of cake baking.

"When you start to smell the cake, you know it is almost done," Mom tells us. Even so, she has set the timer. When it beeps, I hurry to the oven. I peek through the window and see two golden cakes.

"The cakes look perfect!" I call out.

Mom sets the hot pans on the counter to cool.

"Let's get to work on the icing," Sam says.

"And that means it is time for me to leave," Connor tells us.

We all laugh as he hurries out of the kitchen. Then Sam and I mix powdered sugar and butter with cream cheese, vanilla, and a touch of milk.

It is white and creamy. My mouth sort of drools just looking at it.

"Mom, can we try the frosting?" I ask. "You know, to make sure it tastes good?"

Mom doesn't answer but hands us each a spoon. Sam and I dip our spoons into the mixing bowl.

"It's even better than good!" I wish I could eat the whole bowl. But Mom moves it to the counter next to the cake.

We have to wait for the cakes to cool before we can frost them, so Mom takes Abe for a walk, and Sam works on homework. I sit at the table to write my poem for Grandpa. It is about Abe and George and their crazy adventures. My mind starts to wander.

I am at a party, and everyone is all dressed up. Only I am dressed in rags. No one will pay any attention to me. I see Siri, and I wave to her. She pretends not to notice me. Charlotte laughs at me. Even Daisy and Jessica ignore me. I should leave because I am not wanted here. But instead, I walk to the center of the room. And I begin to spin. Around and around. My rags transform into a red-and-blue superhero costume. My secret power is that I can tell when people are being honest with me. Now I will always know the truth.

We finish frosting the cake just before dinner. Then we sprinkle on coconut flakes. I have to admit, it looks exactly like the picture. My poem is finished, and I have written it out on poster board in colored markers. I am really excited to give our gifts to Grandpa.

★ ★ ★

The next morning, we go to church and then run home to pick up Abe and the cake. Grandma and Grandpa only live fifteen minutes away, so by the time Abe squirms from the backseat to the front seat three times, we are there.

Gram flings open the door before we have even piled out of the car. George pushes past her and dashes down the driveway. Abe meets him halfway and they start rolling around, barking and wagging their tails.

The dogs are always so happy to see each other that they barely notice the rest of us. I understand how they feel. I'd really miss my brothers if we had to live in different houses. Mom carries the wrapped cake, and I pull my poster out of the trunk. Sam and Connor have made something together. I don't know what it is though because they say it's a surprise.

"I'm so happy to see all of you!" Gram says as she wraps me in a hug.

"Where's Dad?" my mom asks as she kisses Gram on the cheek.

"In the garage. He's already got the Halloween bins pulled out. I hope you're ready for decorating!"

I glance at Dad. "Try not to get stuck in any trees today."

Dad ruffles my hair. "I'll do my best, but I can't promise anything."

I follow Sam and Connor to the garage. There is my grandfather. Where Gram is sporty, Grandpa is like a television-show grandfather in his sensible blue sweater, khakis, and spectacles.

His white hair always rebels against his smooth hairstyle and pokes up on top, so he has permanent bedhead. He is a history professor so, like me, he loves books.

"Happy birthday!" I call out.

"Oh, thanks for reminding me," Grandpa teases. "I completely forgot about it."

"Dad, you never forget anything," Mom answers as we both hug him at the same time.

"My best girls." Grandpa squeezes us tight. And then he hugs Sam and Connor and Dad. We're kind of a huggy family.

Grandpa notices the poster in my hand. "What do you have there, Ruby?"

"For you," I say as I flip the poster around.

In the center, I have pasted a photo of Abe and George when they were puppies. And below, in different-colored markers, I have written a poem for Grandpa.

Two golden balls of fluff
So innocent and sweet
With their chocolate eyes
And happy smiles
And giant floppy paws
Mischief and mess follow them
Wherever they go
But they are loyal and loving
And make us laugh
No matter what they do
Abe and George
Brothers and friends
We call them family

Grandpa starts clapping, and the rest of my family joins in.

"Paparazzi here!" Gram calls out as she takes my picture with Grandpa.

"Anyone ready for decorating?" Mom asks.

We start looking through the boxes of

Halloween decorations. I choose a set of three giant pumpkins to set up side by side on the grass. Sam helps me drag them to the right spots. Then I stand back and look.

"A little more to the right," I say, my head tilted to the side. Sam pushes the first pumpkin to the right. Then I change my mind. "No, the left. Wait. Maybe back to the right." Sam looks up at me and rolls his eyes. "I'm not doing this on purpose. I mean it," I say, and I do. Something just isn't right.

"Maybe you're missing this," Gram tells us as she sets a pair of Mickey Mouse ears on one of the pumpkins.

I clap my hands together. "That's perfect!"

While Sam and I head back to the boxes for more decorations, Mom helps Dad string lights in the tree.

"Watch out there," Connor calls.

"We don't want a repeat of last year," Sam adds.

"Notice that I am standing on a ladder this time," Dad tells us.

Sam, Connor, and I work on setting up the scarecrow, who looks exactly like the one in *The Wizard of Oz*. Connor and Sam move bales of hay from the garage to make a display in front of the scarecrow. I add the giant sign that reads *Welcome* and is made out of pumpkins. Mom sets a few small pumpkins around the hay bales.

"I almost expect to find the yellow brick road somewhere around here," I tell them.

Mom claps her hands together. "That's a wonderful idea. I bet we could make one."

And we do. Mom draws bricks on white poster boards, and I color them with yellow markers. Sam staples them together so they won't blow away. Then we arrange them to lead right from the scarecrow to the front door.

Pretty soon, Gram calls us all in to lunch. We serve ourselves salads and sandwiches from the dining room table and sit together in the backyard.

Everyone is talking and laughing. Then Connor and Sam bring out Sam's laptop computer and set it on the table in front of Grandpa.

"This is for you," Connor tells him.

"You're giving me a computer?" Grandpa jokes.

"Not the computer," Sam answers. "Look!"

Connor pushes a key, and a title appears on screen.

The Life and Times of William Brook, also known as Grandpa Bill.

My brothers have scanned photos of Grandpa and made them into a movie with music. We see Grandpa at five and thirty-five and in between. The song "Blue Suede Shoes" by Elvis Presley plays as the photos blend, spin, and freeze on screen.

Then we see Gram and Grandpa together in their wedding photo, Grandpa teaching as a professor, and then my mom as a baby. She is standing at the beach holding hands with her little sister and Grandpa. Then we see all four of them on horses. Last, we see the whole family, me included, at Disneyland. We are all wearing Mickey Mouse ears. But I am pretty sure that never actually happened, so Sam and Connor must have used digital graphics to add the ears. Everyone claps—but I clap the loudest. I want to see it again.

"How wonderful!" Gram tells Sam and Connor. Grandpa is actually wiping at his eyes underneath his glasses. I think he might have gotten a little teary, so I slip him a paper napkin without a word. Grandpa takes it and dabs at his eyes.

"That was just beautiful. I have no words," he says. And then everyone laughs because Grandpa is never at a loss for something to say.

Just then, we hear a crash from inside the house. It sounds like breaking glass. Mom is closest to the door, but before she can walk into the house,

Abe and George come running out. They catch Mom by surprise, knocking her sideways. Dad catches her before she falls. The dogs run right underneath the table, yanking the tablecloth and pulling it with them. The dishes and food clatter to the ground. Everyone is shrieking and trying to catch them. But the dogs take off down the side of the house toward the front yard.

"Abe, George—stop!" I call out. But the dogs don't listen.

Sam is fastest, but I am close behind. Everyone else follows us. When we get to the front yard, this is what we see:

A

    ghost

       flying

         through

       the

          pumpkin patch.

This is what it really is:

Abe and George with coconut frosting all over their faces, turning them white and making the tablecloth stick to the tops of their heads so that it streams behind them as they run through the yard.

Mom appears at the front door holding the half-eaten cake. "I hope Abe and George enjoyed the birthday cake."

After all our hard work, no one will even get to try the cake now. I won't get to try the cake now. Then I think about Grandpa. It's his birthday cake after all.

Grandpa is blotting his eyes as he watches the dogs run around in circles trying to get the tablecloth off their heads. I move closer to him. "I'm sorry your birthday is ruined."

"To the contrary, Ruby. This is the best birthday I've ever had," he tells me. That's when I realize he's laughing so hard that he is actually crying. Somehow, that makes it all OK—even better than OK.

Dad pulls out his phone and takes a photo so we can all remember just how the dogs looked in their Halloween costume. I think he is secretly happy to hand over the funniest Halloween story to the dogs. That way, he won't have to hear every year about being stuck in a tree. Now we'll be talking about Abe and George, the frosting ghosts, instead.

CHAPTER 11

The Monday Blues

Monday is my least favorite day of the week because it always seems to take so long to get to Book Club Tuesday.

This Monday is no exception. The day begins with Charlotte giving Siri a glittery heart card with pink feathers glued all around the edges. (It's not that there's anything wrong with giving someone a card. It's actually a pretty nice thing to do, but when that someone is your best friend... Well, let's just say it makes me feel a little sickish inside.)

The day gets worse from there. Mrs. Sablinsky is at jury duty so we have a sub. Some of the subs are really nice, and usually I like having a new teacher for the day. But not this sub. This one can only be described with one word. *Cranky.*

So the super-unfriendliest sub ever—who is named Mrs. Cheer (I'm really and truly serious. That *is* her name!)—starts out by giving us a pop quiz on double-digit division. And then she calls time before I finish the test. That usually never happens to me. When you don't finish a test, you already know you have at least one wrong. And then, as if that wasn't enough, I have to share a book with Will B. I see him stick his finger into his nose and pull something gooey out. Then he actually touches the book *with the same finger*!

By lunchtime, all I can think about is that tomorrow will be Book Club Tuesday. I say it over and over inside my head, like a song. The bell rings, and everyone scrambles out of their seats.

"How do you think you did on the quiz?" Daisy says as we pull our lunches out of our backpacks.

I shrug. "I didn't finish the last question." I'm embarrassed to say it, but it's the truth.

Daisy's eyes widen. "Me either!"

Siri and Charlotte meet up with us on the way to the tables.

"Book club tomorrow," I tell them. "Don't forget to bring one question for the group." Each meeting, we all bring a question to ask the others about the book. Mom's group began this tradition, and she says it really helps to get the conversation started.

Normally, someone would say something about being excited to talk about the book or what kind of cookies they were planning on bringing. Instead, there is silence. I glance over at Siri, eyebrows raised. But she doesn't meet my eyes. Instead, she glances over at Charlotte. Then I look at Daisy, only she doesn't look me in the eye either. I watch as her glance also slides to Charlotte. I am instantly tingling from the top of my head all the way down to my pink laces. It's that feeling you have when you know people have been talking about you when you weren't there.

"Is someone going to tell me what's happening here?" I say these words aloud, even though they are soft. They are so soft that it's like I almost haven't said them at all.

They exchange looks again, and for a split second, I know what it feels like to be Mrs. Cheer. (It's not a super-happy feeling. It's exactly the opposite.)

Finally, Charlotte speaks up. "We're changing the Unicorns to a drama club."

What?

I realize I am blinking really, really fast, almost like my eyelashes are butterfly wings. I can't stop them. "I don't understand," I say, not looking at her, but at Siri.

Siri shrugs, like it doesn't matter. But it matters to me. It matters a whole lot. Then Siri grins a fake smile that doesn't look like her usual smile at all and says, "We all like drama. You do too."

There's something really frustrating about someone telling you that you like something, even if that someone happens to be your best friend and knows that you really do like that something. It's still really frustrating. And that's how I feel right about now.

I shake my head. "That's not the point. You can't just change the Unicorns." This time I am speaking to Charlotte. "We have to vote on it—as a group."

Charlotte juts her chin out and crosses her arms in front of her. "Then vote."

It's a challenge. And as much as I'd like to run away and hide, I don't.

I sit at the lunch table, and my so-called friends sit across from me. Behind me stands a line of girls backing me up. These are my best friends, friends I met in the pages of books. They remind me to be strong and believe in myself. They join hands with one another, making a fence behind me. Jo, Meg, Mary, Hermione, Harriet, India Opal, Dorothy, Alice, and Karana.

I look around at my friends, but none of them will meet my eyes.

"All those in favor of the Unicorns becoming a drama club, raise your hands." Charlotte puts her hand in the air, of course. She's already made her position clear. What I am not prepared for is this:

Siri raises her hand.

Daisy raises her hand.

Jessica doesn't raise her hand. But it's not enough. Charlotte smirks at me.

"Three against two—you lose."

"The Unicorns is a book club, not a drama club," I tell them. "It's like turning a mystery book into a fantasy book. It can't just change like that."

But it's too late. A vote is a vote. Charlotte stands and tilts her head to the side, waiting for the group to fall in line behind her.

I wonder what just happened. How my book club was destroyed in a matter of seconds.

"I thought you liked book club?" I say softly to Siri.

"I do," Siri answers with a quick look at Charlotte. "Sometimes it's nice to try something new."

"Daisy?" I ask. But I know the answer before she speaks.

"It's not personal," Daisy tries to say.

"Sorry, Ruby," Jessica offers. "We tried."

But I shake my head. I don't want to hear any more. I really don't.

And just like that, the Unicorn Book Club is dead.

I sit alone at the lunch table. This is what I have been dreading—the thing I feared the most. All I feel is empty, like I have been hollowed out with an ice-cream scooper. I sit there, staring at the empty lunch bench. And for once, I don't care if I cry in public because the tears wouldn't stop even if I asked them. I don't notice that Will P is sitting next to me until he hands me a wrinkled napkin. I take it and wipe my eyes—then I realize it might be a *used* wrinkled napkin. *Ewwwww!* I hand it back, now wet with tears.

"Thanks."

"Do you want to talk about it?" he asks. I shrug. If I speak, the window will open and the tears will flow through again. Instead, I look down at his socks. Today Will is wearing bright-yellow socks with life-size grasshoppers all over them. For a split second, the socks make me forget everything.

Then Will says, "It's the book club, isn't it?" I manage a small nod. Will shrugs, "I heard Charlotte and Siri talking. So I guess they want to focus on drama instead of reading."

I sniffle a little at that. The way Will tells it, the situation sounds way more straightforward. It doesn't seem like I just lost all my friends. It seems more like they want to try another activity. I wish that were true.

"I like reading," Will offers. "Maybe *I* could be in your book club."

It's not a bad idea, actually. Instead of sitting here feeling sorry for myself, I could start a new book club. It seems very Nancy Drew of me, not to wallow but to move forward.

"Would you really want to be in my book club?" I ask him. "Really?"

Will nods. "Just one thing though." He holds up his hand to stop me. "We have to change the name. I'm not going to be in the Unicorns. Way too girlie."

"Unicorns aren't girlie at all," I argue. "Maybe the ones you see on stickers with pink horns and purple sparkly tails. But not the magical ones, not the Harry Potter–style unicorns."

Will just watches me with one eyebrow raised. But the truth is, even if I could convince him to become a Unicorn, I can't use the name. The Unicorns have moved on without me. "I guess we can pick a new name. Any ideas?"

"Polar Bears," Will says. "I want to be the Polar Bears Book Club."

"I like polar bears," I say. "But I like other bears too. Why them?"

Will sits up straighter in his seat, pushes his glasses up on his nose, and takes a giant breath.

"Polar bears are at the top of the food chain, live exclusively in the Arctic, and are the largest land carnivores in the world. They are classified as marine mammals because they spend so much time in the water. Most importantly, experts believe that polar bears are in danger of becoming extinct in the next fifty years because of the loss of sea ice. As an added bonus, they are extremely cute. Need I say more?"

It is impossible not to like Will P. He is just that kind of person, the kind that can make you smile even when you are having the worst day of your life. So that's what I do right now. I smile. "OK, Will. Polar Bears win."

Will claps his hands together. "Wondermazing! Now, what do you actually *do* at a book club?"

"The best part about book club is that we are all reading the same book at the same time. It's fun because we can share ideas and thoughts about the story and characters. Everyone gets to ask one question of the group to get the discussion started. Like, 'Why do you think Winn–Dixie ran away?' Something like that. Oh, and we share lunch just like we share ideas."

Will nods, "Got it."

I think of something then. We don't have a book to read. "Will, we need to choose a book, even if we don't have time to read it. So we can at least have something to talk about."

Will offers me half a chocolate-chip cookie. I don't have much of an appetite, but the friendly thing to do is to at least take the cookie. So I do.

I expect this to take a really long time, but he manages on the first try.

"*The Secret Merlin Society.*"

My grin almost cracks my face in two, and I nearly fall right off the bench. I am that excited. *The Secret Merlin Society* is a brand-new book about a group of kids in sixth grade who have a secret society where they perform magic to save the world. "That's a super-fantastical choice, Will."

Will grins back at me. "You used my word, *fantastical*. Don't worry. I'll let you borrow it. Oh, can I bring some friends too?"

I shrug. "The more the merrier, isn't that what they say?" A teeny-weeny voice inside my head says, "Not so fast, Starr. You might be making one ginormous mistake." OK, maybe the voice isn't really so teeny-weeny. Maybe it's actually screaming in my ear. But it's too late, because Will has already run off to find his friends and tell them about the Polar Bears. No, this will have to be what my dad calls "a learning experience," which is another word for making a lowercase *m* mistake and then having to make the best of it.

My happiness at being part of a new book club doesn't help me with the stomach jitters that attack for the rest of the school day. Daisy and Jessica go out of their way to be really nice to me. It's like they know how bad they made me feel and are trying to fix it. Somehow, even though it shouldn't, their niceness makes me feel worse. Siri barely makes eye contact. And during the last hour of class, when Mrs. Cheer lets us work on a word search with partners, Siri goes to Charlotte's desk without even looking my way. I know because I watch her the entire time. I work by myself. Sometimes it's easier to be alone than to pretend with someone else.

In my hand, I hold a small glass jar filled with sparkly gold dust. It can make any wish come true. I make my wish: to be completely and totally invisible. I open the jar and pour the dust over my head. Instantly, I disappear. My green sneakers are all that remain to show where I am. The worst part is, no one even notices that I am gone.

CHAPTER 12

The Lowercase *m* Mistake

When the bell finally rings and I can escape, I grab my backpack without talking to anyone. Mrs. Cheer stands at the doorway, waving good-bye to us with a pretend smile on her face. But I know she is secretly thrilled that this day is finally over, and she can go home. Mrs. Cheer and I have a lot in common at the moment. Because I am thrilled that this day is finally over too. I run to the front of school to meet Gram. I run like I am being chased by a wicked witch on a broom: super-duper, extra-speedy fast.

"Hi, pumpkin," Gram calls out. Her arms are open wide for a hug even before I reach them. I crash right into her, nearly knocking her over. Then I nestle into her red sweater for a few seconds, but that's all. I know if I let myself stay in her hug for too long, I will be a puddle of embarrassment on the front lawn of school. Instead, I pull away and take her hand.

"Can we go to the library?" I ask her.

"My favorite place," she answers as she takes my backpack and slings it over her shoulder. "I'd love to."

On the way, I fill her in on the details of the Very Horrible Day (which is what I have named today). She laughs when I tell her about Mrs. Cheer and then frowns when she hears about the destruction of the Unicorn Book Club.

"I'm making lemonade, Gram," I tell her. "That's what I am doing." I am taking the lemons Siri and the other girls have handed me. And I am turning them into something sweet—a new book club.

Gram is pulling Grambus into a parking space at the library. She turns to grin at me. "You can see a glass as half-full or half-empty, pumpkin. It's all completely up to you. Myself, I choose the half-full every time."

"I hope we can find the book I need for tomorrow. I want to get started on the first chapter at least." Mrs. Cheer didn't give us any homework tonight so I have lots of time to read.

We head straight for the children's library on the right side. It's behind an open archway entirely made out of wooden books. And the best part is that all the wooden books have titles. They aren't just fake-to-look-real books. All the classics are represented: *Peter Pan*, *The Secret Garden*, *Little Women*, *Black Beauty*, *Grimm's Fairy Tales*. So when I pass underneath the archway, it's like I am being welcomed by my oldest friends.

My favorite librarian is Miss Mary. She is in college, studying to be a teacher. So she works at the library in the afternoons. The best thing about Miss Mary is that she knows every book in the entire children's library. Seriously, she has read every single one—which is pretty amazing since there must be thousands and thousands of books here.

"Miss Mary!" I whisper, excited to see her curly brown hair and big smile.

"Hi there, Ruby. How's my favorite reader?"

"Actually, it's been kind of a tough day so far. I've actually named it 'the Very Horrible Day.'"

Miss Mary scrunches up her nose, which makes her look even younger than she usually does. "I'm sorry, Ruby. That's not what I like to hear. But you know, there's one thing that can always make a bad day better—books."

I grin at her. Book people understand one another. I know exactly what Miss Mary means. You can lose yourself in a book. That's the absolute best thing about reading.

"I'm looking for a particular book today," I

tell her. I would love nothing more than to roam the shelves and find a book that no one (except Miss Mary) even knows is here. But today, I am on a mission. *"The Secret Merlin Society."*

Miss Mary's eyes twinkle, and she smiles really big. "Best book ever. It's definitely in my Top Ten Favorites of All Time category."

I turn to grin at Gram, and she winks at me. Suddenly, the day isn't so completely horrible after all. Only, just then, Miss Mary says these words:

"But I'm not sure we have a copy right now."

"She needs it for a book club meeting tomorrow," Gram explains.

"I understand," Miss Mary says, puckering her lips. "Let me do some checking. Just give me a couple of minutes."

Gram offers to help me choose another book. But I don't want to look for another book when I need this one. It seems disloyal somehow. So instead, I sit down on the yellow-and-white polka-dot chair in the corner. Gram sits on the blue-and-yellow-striped sofa. And we wait.

I can see Miss Mary from where I am sitting. First, she types on the computer. Next, she picks up the telephone. Then, she searches the back shelves. How many places can one middle-grade book hide? Finally, she comes over to us.

"So here's the thing, I have good news and bad news."

I'd rather have the bad news first, to get it out of the way and all. But she gives me the good first.

"The good news is that we have one copy here in the library."

I smile.

"The bad news is that I can't seem to locate it."

And the frown is back.

"But don't worry, Ruby. It has to be here somewhere. It's just been misfiled or pulled for some reason. I am going to look now."

Miss Mary disappears into the main part of

the library. I can see her talking to another librarian. They turn back to look at me, so I know they are talking about me. Then that librarian walks with Miss Mary to a third librarian. Soon, there are five librarians searching for my book.

It should make me feel good that so many people are trying to help me. But it doesn't. It actually makes me feel bad that they are all looking for this book for me. And that I am causing them so much trouble. Because if the Unicorns were still a book club, like they were supposed to be, I wouldn't be rushing out at the last minute trying to find a book. I would already have the book, and no one would have to work so hard to help me.

My eyes start stinging a little bit at that last thought. Gram must realize because she moves over to stand beside me. She reaches out and touches the top of my head.

"Give them a few more minutes. I think they'll find it for you."

I know that a minute is only sixty seconds, and a *few* is about three minutes. So altogether, a few minutes should only be one hundred and eighty seconds, which really isn't that long. But it seems like a thousand minutes go by before Miss Mary returns.

"Only good news this time, Ruby," she says as she holds up a copy of *The Secret Merlin Society* with the society's symbol of stars in the shape of a sword on the cover.

I can't help myself. I know I am in fifth grade and all, but I jump up and down and squeal like I have just won a trip to Disney World. I'm that happy. I hug Miss Mary. Then I hug Gram. Then I hug both Miss Mary and Gram.

"Thank you, thank you, thank you. This is the best day ever!" I tell them.

"I'm so happy to know that we're past the Very Horrible Day," Gram responds with a grin.

"Oh, that's ancient history." I return her

smile with a giant one of my own. "I can't wait to start reading right away. Right this very minute." I plop down on the blue-and-yellow-striped sofa and open to page one.

"Not so fast," Gram says with a wink. "We're out of time. We have to go get your brothers now."

I sigh. Page one of *The Secret Merlin Society* will have to wait just a little bit longer.

Gram turns back to Miss Mary and thanks her again for all her help. "You have been a real lifesaver today."

"A superhero of extraordinary powers," I add. "I'll let you know how the first meeting of the Polar Bears Book Club goes tomorrow."

"I can't wait to hear," Miss Mary tells us.

Then I follow Gram through the library and out the door, cradling the book like a baby kitten the entire way home.

★ ★ ★

By morning, I have read all of chapter one and half of chapter two. I am thrilled to report that the girl in the story, Navera, is the most powerful of all the magicians. The society meets in a secret basement underneath the oldest library in their town, and they wear special golden rings to connect with each other.

I can't wait to discuss this with Will P at lunch. I even pack extra cookies and raisins to share with the group.

When I arrive at school, I don't go over to Siri and the other Unicorns like I usually would. I am giving them the Shun. The Shun is when someone close to you is mad at you, and they decide to shun or ignore you like you smell bad or something.

I have nothing to say to any of them (except maybe Jessica because she did vote for the Unicorns to stay as a book club). Charlotte must not understand the Shun though. Because she actually comes and stands next to me in line.

"Hi, Ruby. I like your dress." Today is Picture Day, so I am wearing a pink dress with green and white flowers on it. My hair is in two ponytails that kind of bounce around 'cause of the curls. Of course, I have on my green sneakers with the pink laces. They go perfectly with everything.

It's an upside-down, backward sort of day: giving the Shun to Siri and receiving a compliment from Charlotte.

"Thanks," I mumble. "I like yours too."

Charlotte smiles at me, a real smile that even shows her braces. And then I realize. Charlotte is the only one who is happy I am not part of the Unicorn Drama Club, because now she can have the Unicorns all for herself. And by Unicorns, I don't just mean the book club part of the Unicorns; I mean the members of the Unicorns also known as my friends.

Charlotte is wearing a striped dress. Her hair is brushed out long, and she has a red ribbon tied around her head like a headband. I figure even though I know her niceness isn't really coming from the heart, I shouldn't let on that I know. Maybe sometimes it's better just to pretend. So I smile back and compliment her outfit too. "Red looks nice on you."

The compliment is out of my mouth before I can stop it. What am I doing? I am being nice to the enemy!

"At my old school, they let us hold a special item in our class pictures," Charlotte tells me. (If her wonderful old school was so fantastic, why didn't she just stay there?)

I have no comment to make. What can I say anyway? *How terrific that your old school was so much better than ours. But you're stuck here now, so you might as well make the best of it.* Or, *Wow, I wish I could go there. You are so completely and totally lucky, Charlotte.*

Instead, I try to smile. My lips curve up, but

the frown pushes down. Up, down. Up, down. In the end, the frown presses the smile into a straight line. So that is the expression I turn toward Charlotte.

"You would probably hold a book, I'm guessing," Charlotte says with her chin jutting out toward me. Before I can even think of a comeback, Charlotte moves ahead of me to follow Mrs. Cheer into the classroom. Yep, that's right. Mrs. Cheer is back for Day Two. As I pass Mrs. Cheer at the door, I can positively say that my expression and her expression are the same. And that neither one of us wants to be here right now.

CHAPTER 13

The Lowercase *m* Mistake Has a Sequel

Will P stops by my desk first thing. He points to his socks. They are bright red with books all over them. For a moment, the socks make me so happy that I forget about everything else.

"Will, I absolutely and completely *love* your socks!" I tell him.

Will poses in them like he is in a fashion show. "I'm fantastically stylish, Ruby. It's one of my gifts," he tells me and then hurries away to take his seat before Mrs. Cheer marks his name on the board.

That's Mrs. Cheer's revenge. She writes on the board the name of every person who doesn't behave perfectly. And when I say perfectly, I mean hands folded in lap, eyes on the board perfectly. That way, Mrs. Sablinsky can "deal" with us when she gets back. So far, my name is not on the list. Siri and Charlotte have both made the board though—for talking. I have to look at their names written there in red, side by side. It almost looks like an advertisement for the new BFFs in class. *Siri and Charlotte.*

After we read a chapter of social studies out loud, Mrs. Cheer tells us to line up at the door.

"It's time for your class pictures," she announces. I wonder if substitute teachers get to stand in for the teacher in the class picture. I imagine Mrs. Cheer and I could stand side by side, with our matching upside-down smiles (a.k.a. frowns).

We walk in a single-file line to the auditorium, which would normally make me really unhappy because I couldn't talk to my friends.

Today, it feels like a little surprise, like spotting a monarch butterfly gliding past.

"Please line yourselves up in height order," Mrs. Cheer tells us when we arrive outside the auditorium. Everyone scurries around, arguing about who is taller. I just find a place between two people I barely know.

Someone passes me a basket with tiny plastic combs. If we need to fix our hair, we can take one. My hair is too curly to even try one of the combs. I would either break it or end up with the comb knotted in my hair.

I see my class photo in a fancy golden frame hanging on a museum wall. A crowd stands in front to look. The caption underneath my photo reads: "Princess Ruby, Age 10." And there I am, wearing a ruby tiara and a strand of pearls and diamonds around my neck. Only a black plastic comb is stuck in my curls, and I have a giant frown on my face. The crowd points and laughs at my horrifically awful class picture. Their cameras flash as they take pictures.

Flash. My eyes blink as I realize the camera flash is real.

I quickly put on my best picture smile. I've been perfecting this one since I was four.

"That's it. You're all finished. Next..." The photographer shoos me away and turns to the next person in line.

I stand to the side, waiting for the rest of the line to finish. Some of the boys are sword fighting with the combs. Daisy and Jessica are braiding each other's hair. I refuse to even look at Charlotte and Siri. So I tie and retie my shoes as long as possible. And then I play with the ruffles on my dress. I multiply the number of ruffles times the number of flowers. Then I divide. Then I add them together, and then I subtract. Math is my new best friend.

"Time for the class photo," Mrs. Cheer finally says. It is with relief that I follow her to the front of school where we line up in the same height order to take our class photo. I notice that Mrs. Cheer isn't allowed in the picture. Her face doesn't look all cranky just then. In fact, I think it might look almost sad. I know how it feels to not belong.

"You can go outside for a half-hour break," Mrs. Cheer tells us. Mrs. Sablinsky never gives us breaks like this. I'm guessing Mrs. Cheer needs the break more than we do.

Everyone runs across the yard. I walk. I have nowhere I need to be.

Jessica moves next to me. "I'm sure you're really sad about the book club. *I* am. I just wanted you to know that," she tells me in a quiet voice.

When someone does something really truly nice, it takes your breath away. That's what happens to me when Jessica talks to me. I lose my breath.

"I know," I tell her. "But I don't want the Unicorns to be a drama club. That's not why we started it."

Jessica nods like she agrees. But she doesn't say it out loud.

"Wanna sit with us at lunch?" she asks.

I want to say *yes*, I really do. But I'm giving the Shun to Siri, even if I'm not giving it to Jessica. And when you are giving the Shun to someone, you don't eat lunch with them.

So that's why I answer like this: "Not today, Jessica. But thank you."

★ ★ ★

And that's how I end up spending my free time with Mrs. Xia in the library. It's not that I'm afraid to make new friends. I'm not. I try walking around the yard once. I even see some girls I might want to get to know better. But the truth is that when people are already grouped together, it's hard to join. Not impossible, just hard. So I pretend like I am just walking to the library. And that was my plan all along. Only I know the truth.

"Welcome!" Mrs. Xia says as I walk through the door. "What are you reading today?"

"*The Secret Merlin Society*," I answer with a smile. I know she will love this choice. And I am right. Because Mrs. Xia claps her hands together.

"Wonderful! Such an exciting adventure. I'd like to be in the Society myself."

"Me too," I tell her. "And I'm only on the second chapter."

Mrs. Xia chats with me about—what else?—*books* and then puts me right to work.

"You can reshelve all these books. The first graders returned them this morning, and I haven't had a chance to put them back."

I breathe in the smell of the library—old books and new books. It is comforting and exciting at the same time. Old friends and new friends are all gathered in this place. Then I stack the books really tall and lift them into my arms. I can't see over the top, so I have to crane my neck to the side. If my mom were here, she would ask me to put half of them down and make two trips. But Mrs. Xia is at her computer tapping away on the keys. And she doesn't see.

I make my way to the fiction section and set the stack of books on the round red table in front of the bookshelves. I look at the titles wistfully as I put each one away. These are some of my favorite books. And I can still remember my excitement at finishing a whole story all by myself. I open the books and read a few pages of each, sort of like saying hello to old friends.

I open a book and look down at the page. I see a picture
of a meadow. Suddenly, I am inside the meadow. I have
stepped right into the book. A white horse with a pink
mane and tail gallops out of the trees and comes to stand
beside me. I have read this story before, and the horse is an
old friend. He lets me ride him around the meadow. Then
we collect wildflowers to braid in his tail. I wish I could
stay, but I know I am only visiting.

★ ★ ★

Time flies quickly in the library, almost at warp speed. Before I know it, the half hour is over.

"Thank you for your help today, Ruby," Mrs. Xia tells me as she offers me a present from her treasure box. I'd like to say I am too old for these things. At the dentist I usually refuse a prize, now that I am ten and all. But Mrs. Xia has book-related prizes, and many of them are really, really old. I choose a bookmark from the nineteen-fifties with a small Scottie dog holding a book in his mouth. Underneath the dog in bright-red letters it says, *Reading Makes Me Happy.*

Four words have never been so true. Because I leave the library with a smile on my face.

Back in class, I am still giving Siri the Shun, and now I have added Charlotte too. So even though my table, Table 3, is assigned to study social studies with Table 1 (Siri's table) and Table 5 (Charlotte's table), I avoid making eye contact or even speaking to them. I answer questions and work with the other students, but I act like Siri and Charlotte are completely and totally invisible.

When lunch arrives, Will P meets me at the backpacks.

"Ready for book club?" he asks.

I grin and nod. *I'm making lemonade*, I remind myself. On the way, I tell him about my library adventure yesterday and the search for the missing book. Will P is a great audience. He listens to my story and smiles at all the right parts.

When we arrive at the lunch tables, I notice that the Unicorns are sitting at a different table than our usual one. They are all the way across the yard. I try not to let it bother me. I really and truly do. But it does. It tugs on my heart, like it's stretching it to pull off a piece, like you do with licorice. You have to pull and stretch it before it breaks off.

I sit down across from Will P and pull out my cloth napkin. I lay it on the table and put my lunch on it: a turkey sandwich cut into squares in a wax-paper wrapping, mini oatmeal cookies in a small reusable container, and red grapes in a small round tin. Will P adds his lunch: a quesadilla cut into small wedges, tortilla chips in a bag, and pickles in a tiny plastic container.

"Welcome to the first meeting of the Polar Bears Book Club!" Will P announces.

I think it's just going to be the two of us. And that's really OK with me. I'm actually kind of happy about it. Only just then five boys start scooting into the seats next to us. The boys that like to throw things. The boys that like to fake vomit. Will B squeezes in right next to me. Will B!

"We have to share our lunches," Will P reminds them. But instead of laying the food out neatly as we have done, the boys just begin dumping their lunches onto the napkin. Pieces of sugary cereal shower onto my sandwich. Orange slices plop on the cereal. Then someone actually puts a tuna sandwich on top of that. My red grapes are nowhere to be seen. I watch, horrified, as the boys begin scarfing up the food. They push and shove until the whole lunch is just a mushed-up, mixed-up mess. And that pretty much exactly describes me.

I look over at Will P and raise my eyebrows. Will P shrugs at me, as if to say "sorry." There is no possible way we can have a book club meeting like this. I open my mouth to tell Will P that the first meeting of the Polar Bears is officially canceled. And a grape lands on my tongue! A grape covered in tuna fish, sugary cereal, orange slices, and maybe even pickle.

EWWWWWWWWWWWWWWWWWWWWW WWWWWWWWWWWWWWWWWWWWW!

The Polar Bears Book Club is now a food fight club. I spit the disgusting grape out into my hand and wipe off my tongue with a napkin. For a split second, I consider throwing the grape right at Will P. But I don't. Because this isn't his fault— it's mine. I said he could invite friends, and I knew when I said it that I was making a mistake. Now I am sure I made a mistake.

So I calmly stand up, and with my lunch bag in one hand and my book in the other, walk away from the table. I stop when I feel something hit the back of my head. But I don't turn around. I just keep walking. Within seconds, I hear the lunch aide blow her whistle and order the boys to clean up their mess.

My head suddenly seems swollen, as if it's a giant balloon that is going to lift me into the sky so I can fly away from here. Then I realize it's because my eyes are filled with tears. I sniffle them back and swallow hard. I want to go to the nurse's office and tell her I have a bad stomachache. (It wouldn't even be a lie. My stomach does really hurt.)

But I don't. Because my favorite characters never run away from their problems. They face them. And when they try something and it doesn't work, well, they try something else. I thought the Polar Bears would be a solution to my problem. But it only made my problem worse. Because the Polar Bears made it more obvious that I am completely and totally alone.

CHAPTER 14

An Unexpected Twist

On Wednesday morning, I try everything to stay home from school. I begin with the most reliable argument, the stomachache. This is the most reliable because:

1. It is true; I do have a stomachache, and truth has rightness on its side.
2. Mom can't measure it like a fever or a cough or stuffy nose. (I mean, no one can deny when a stuffy nose is really and truly stuffy.)

When that fails, I move on to the next best argument, the Shun. This is powerful because it is true, and it is painful at the same time, as painful as skinning your knee on gravel.

But instead of getting a day home from school, I get a talk about friendship. (A talk isn't like a lecture. It's friendlier, like a "we're in this together" conversation. But it still takes a long time and sort of feels like a lecture even if it isn't.) Mom disagrees with my Polar Bears/Shun approach.

"Ruby, I'm so sorry this has been so hard for you. Sometimes as you start to get older, you find that you and your friends have different interests. And that might mean it's time to find some new friends."

Hearing her say it out loud makes my stomach hurt even more. Mom runs her hand over my curls and pulls me close to her.

"I admire you for staying true to yourself. I never want you to be the kind of person who follows along without thinking for herself. But you can't replace your best friends by creating a new book club. Friendships take time and effort. It might be time to make some new friends, but you can't just order them up like fast food." She sighs. "Ignoring Siri isn't the best way to express your feelings. It's always better to talk about it." Mom is usually right about friend stuff. And I know she is right about this. I just don't like to admit it.

Plus, this talk is doing nothing to bring me closer to my goal of staying home from school today. So, I have to resort to the last possible choice on my list: tears. The tears that flow from my eyes are as large as dragon tears. And Mom holds me close. She even calls for Dad. Both of them sit on my bed and hold me tight.

"Friend troubles," Mom whispers to Dad. But I can still hear her.

I sniffle and wipe my nose on the arm of my cupcake pajamas. Mental note to self: put pj's into the laundry basket ASAP.

"So I can stay home today?" My voice is really, really tiny and squeaky.

Mom and Dad look at one another, and their eyes talk to each other. Then Dad turns to me and says, "Ruby, staying home would be like giving up."

"Like running away," Mom adds.

"And you can't run away from your problems," Dad finishes.

I sigh. "So I have to go." It's not a question. It's a statement. None of my ideas worked, and my parents are sending me to school, even though yesterday was probably the worst, most awful day of my entire life. Maybe my parents think this is the right thing to do, but they are wrong. This is the worst possible choice they could make. And I tell them.

"You're sending me to school, knowing it will be misery for me. Knowing that I might possibly have the worst day of my life. And still, you're sending me." These are the words I say, in between sniffles.

Mom and Dad look at each other again so their eyes can talk. I hold my breath. Maybe they are changing their minds.

"Ruby, maybe I should call Siri's mom. Get you girls together to work this out," Mom suggests.

And it's like a bee has just landed on me because I leap out of bed, my hands flailing in the air. "Absolutely. Not. The. Right. Choice!" I tell her. "Siri isn't the problem. Charlotte is. And you can't exactly call up a parent you don't even know. Besides, I don't have her phone number."

"Well, that's easy enough to get," Dad says. "We can also talk to Mrs. Sablinsky. Maybe she can help."

This is getting worse by the minute. "No, no, no!" I rant as I pace around the room. My hands are all sweaty, and my forehead actually feels like someone is painting it with warm water. "You don't understand. I need to switch schools. I need to homeschool. Talking to people isn't going to help anything. I thought you understood." Now I start to cry really and truly for real, more for real than any crying I have done in my entire ten years of life.

Mom stands and wraps her arms around me. I stop pacing and let her hold me. My tears sink into her work shirt. "Ruby, we're just trying to help. We have to find a solution here. And leaving school is not an option."

Just then, Connor comes into the room, followed by Sam. Now the whole entire family is crowded into my book-filled bedroom.

"What's wrong, Ruby?" Sam asks while Connor grabs my hand. I shrug. Having a family that cares about you helps. But they can't go with me to school, even though I wish they could.

"Friend troubles," Dad tells them.

"You need to do the invisible-wall trick," Sam says.

"Absolutely. Works every time," Connor adds.

"I forgot about that," Dad says.

My head slowly lifts from Mom's shirt as I turn to look at my brothers. "What's the invisible-wall trick?" I ask them.

"You're having problems with people hurting your feelings, right?" Sam asks. I nod.

"Right, so what you need is a wall between you and them, so you can get through your day," Connor tells me.

"Only you have to imagine it," they say at the same time.

Imagining I can do. I am the Queen of Imagination.

"So pretend there is an invisible wall between you and them. You can see other people. But nothing they do can get to you. It's stopped by the wall," Sam finishes.

"And that way, you can just get through your day," Connor says.

I think about this. An invisible wall between me and the Unicorns. It just might work.

I nod at them. "I'll try it."

Everybody in my family starts cheering then. And they all hug me at once. Even Abe manages

to squeeze into the circle. I'm a Ruby sandwich.
And I like it. I like it a lot.

★ ★ ★

I think about the invisible wall all the way to school.

I imagine see-through bricks stacking one on top of another
to build a circle around me, like a turret on a castle. I am in
the middle, and I am completely and totally safe. Nothing
can harm me here. I can dance around, and no one can even
say anything rude about it.

Mrs. Sablinsky is back, which is good and bad. It's good because now our schedule is back to normal, and bad because she's really revved up from two days sitting in a courtroom. She piles the work on us from the moment we step into the classroom. I barely have time to think about the Unicorns. (I barely have time to swallow.)

Just before lunch, Mrs. Sablinsky asks if any of the yard guards would like to take an extra shift, because Bethany is absent today. I raise my hand and sit up really tall in my seat. I resist the urge to wave my hand around and bounce up and down to draw attention to myself because I know Mrs. Sablinsky can't stand it.

"I see one person quietly raising her hand, without shouting or waving and carrying on. So, Ruby Starr, you may go help today."

Out of all the kids raising their hands, Mrs. Sablinsky chose me. Me! Ruby Starr!

I hurry to get a yard guard badge out of the

drawer and grab my lunch. Everyone else in class is going to be watching a video on the Statue of Liberty. We have seen two of these already, and they are so old I bet they showed them when my grandma was in school. They are all black-and-white and grainy. And the sound comes out warbled like it's been run through the washing machine. So I know everyone in class wishes they were me right now, even Charlotte Thomas.

Bethany's partner is a girl from the other fifth-grade class. Her name is Charissa, and she's nice but super shy. She smiles at me without using her teeth. It's what I call a shy smile. But that's fine by me. Any smile today is a good thing.

We help the kindergarten kids. They are so adorable that I forget about all my problems for a little while. Instead, I help push a little girl on the swing. I tie a boy's sneakers. And I play hide-and-seek with a pair of twins in matching pink cowboy boots.

"This was fun," I tell Charissa as we walk to the lunch tables. "I like the kindergarten yard."

"I know. They are really cute, aren't they?" she says. And this time, she gives me a real and true smile. "Want to sit together?" she asks me then.

"Definitely," I tell her. I can't wait to tell Mom that I made a new friend today. And even better, her lunch group is the group of girls I wanted to get to know better. They make room for me and Charissa. We say hi, and all of them—every single girl at the table—smiles at me.

That's when I remember that Charissa and I are still wearing our yard guard badges. We are supposed to return them to the classrooms as soon as we finish our shifts.

"Charissa, I'll take your badge for you. I'll be right back," I tell her. The aides on the yard let me cross back over the red lines. I go to Charissa's class first. The door to Room 16 is open, so I leave the badge in the drawer. No one is around when I get to Room 15, and the door is closed. I imagine Mrs. Sablinsky has gone to the teachers' lounge to eat her lunch. For a split second, my mind wanders, and I think about what Mrs. Sablinsky eats for lunch every day. I bet she eats something really sensible, like peapods or trail mix. This is what I am thinking about as I open the door to Room 15. I don't notice at first that Mrs. Sablinsky is still in the room. But then I hear her speaking. I stop in my tracks as I see she is having a meeting with someone. There is only one reason someone has to stay in at lunchtime to meet with the teacher.

You have to be in some kind of trouble.

So I know I shouldn't be here, even though it isn't my fault that I'm here. I am bringing back the yard guard badge, and this is an acceptable reason to return to the classroom. Only now I'm not sure what to do. How I wish I had that invisibility cloak right about now!

I also wish I could un-hear what I am

hearing. Because Mrs. Sablinsky hasn't noticed that I am in the room so she is still talking. She is sitting at her desk on the other side of the classroom. And the student standing in front of Mrs. Sablinsky with her back to me is none other than Charlotte Thomas.

"I've called your father to talk about this, but I want to let you know that I am going to recommend a special teacher to help you with your reading once a day. I don't know how your other school didn't catch this, but you are behind. Maybe two grade levels. We need to catch you up before sixth grade. So you're going to have to work extra hard, but I know you can do it."

Charlotte has a problem with reading. Two grade levels behind means she is reading at a third-grade level. My heart opens just a tiny bit. Enough to understand that Charlotte might not be as perfect as she pretends. Suddenly, everything makes sense.

That's when Mrs. Sablinsky notices me. Her head lifts as she sees me.

"Ruby, we are having a private meeting in here."

Charlotte turns around, and even from the other side of the room, I can see she is crying. Her face is all red, and her eyes look puffy.

"I'm so sorry, Mrs. Sablinsky. I didn't know. I was returning this." I hold up the badge to prove to her that I am not some kind of snoop.

Mrs. Sablinsky sighs. She always sighs when she talks to me. "Very well. Put the badge away, but be quick about it. I need to finish speaking to Charlotte."

That's when I open my mouth and speak without thinking. I know it's one of my worst habits, and it usually gets me in a lot of lowercase *t* trouble. But I do it anyway.

"I can help Charlotte."

What? I can't believe I have just spoken

those four words. What in the world is wrong with me?

Mrs. Sablinsky tilts her head to the side, and for a split second, she reminds me of Abe, when I'm asking him to do something and he isn't quite sure what. He tilts his head to the side, like tilting helps his brain to work better or something. That's exactly what Mrs. S does.

Then I look at Charlotte. Her eyes are all watery, but I can still see surprise in them. Her mouth flattens into a straight line, and I can tell she is worried about this. And that she doesn't like it one bit. For some reason, this makes me speak up even louder.

"I will be her tutor. If she wants."

CHAPTER 15

Making Changes for Real

So that's how I end up in the library at lunch introducing Charlotte to Mrs. Xia. I take Charlotte to the shelf of books that holds my absolute favorites, the ones I was so proud to finally finish all on my own.

"Charlotte, I want you to meet some of my best and truest friends. They will be your best friends too. If you let them," I tell her with a grin.

Because something truly amazing has happened to me today. I am no longer afraid of Charlotte Thomas. I am no longer jealous of Charlotte Thomas. I now understand that she hates books because she can't really read them, not all by herself. So she has never been able to get lost in a story or become best friends with a main character. She has never been able to fall asleep dreaming of a new ending to her favorite book, one where she becomes the lead character. She has never finished a book just to reread it all over again. And this has made me want to help her. Because I know I can. I didn't need the invisible wall after all.

"How can books be your friends?" Charlotte asks. She still looks surprised to be here in the library, with me of all people.

"Well, it's not the books so much as the characters inside the books," I explain. "When I read a book to myself, I can hear the character's voices in my head. And they come alive to me. So it feels like they are real, and that I know them. It's like no one else in the world can see them exactly the way I do, because I imagine them and no one else can see inside my imagination."

I am in the empty white room again. The three doors are
before me: one red, one blue, and one green. This time, I
open the red door. Inside is a fire pit full of anger. I open
my mouth and scream. All the mad feelings I have about
Charlotte explode from inside me. I am a fire-breathing
princess, half human and half dragon. Fire arcs from my
mouth to join the fire inside the room. It blends in and
disappears. I am left open and ready to fill my heart with
something else. Compassion.

I take one of my favorite books off the shelf. It is a story about a girl who rescues a dog from the pound, but then the dog rescues her right back.

"I think you might like this one," I tell her. "We can read the words together, and I'll help you when you can't get one."

Charlotte's eyes meet mine. "Why are you doing this? So you can tell everyone how stupid I am?" Her voice is almost a whisper, and she is blinking back tears.

I shake my head. "I'm doing this because books are everything to me. I thought you didn't like books because you didn't like me. But now I realize it's the other way around. You didn't like me because you don't like books. But not for long."

I hand her the book about the girl and the dog. She takes it from me, but she is still waiting for me to tell her something. I know what that something is.

"I'm not going to tell anyone anything," I say. "It's your secret to tell. But maybe you should trust your friends with the truth."

Charlotte sighs and opens the first page of the book. "Don't laugh," she tells me with narrowed eyes.

"I promise," I tell her. "You know, my mom told me something that might help you. I know it helped me a lot. She said, 'You can do anything you want to do—as long as you believe in yourself.' And I know you can read really well, Charlotte. But you have to believe in yourself."

Charlotte nods at me. And then she starts to read. She messes up a lot of the words. But I help her. And we get through the whole first chapter before the bell rings.

On the way back to class, Charlotte reaches out and touches my shoulder.

"This is the first time in my life I've ever liked a book," she says softly.

I smile at her. "And this is just the beginning."

"I'm sorry I changed the Unicorns to a drama club. It was your group, and I messed it up." She looks down at the ground at this last part.

"Maybe we can have Drama Club Thursdays instead," I say. As long as my Book Club Tuesdays are back, I don't mind trying something new on another day.

She nods. Then Charlotte tosses her dark hair over her shoulder and smirks at me before saying, "Maybe I'll even have to dress up as a character from a book for Halloween."

"That's my thing!" I say, only I am smiling.

"Yeah, I know," she answers, smiling back.

★ ★ ★

After school, I tell Mom all about my day.

"I am so proud of you," she tells me. "Why don't you invite Charlotte over on Friday after school?"

I think about that. It's one thing to help Charlotte at school, but do I really want to let her come to my home?

"I think she would probably relax a lot more if she didn't think someone could hear her make a mistake," Mom offers.

"Maybe," I say. "Do you think she will make fun of me? Like tease me about how many books I have in my room or something like that?"

Mom runs her hand over my head, smoothing my hair back from my forehead. "You can't be afraid of things that *might* happen. You just have to take steps forward. What would you do if she made fun of your books?"

I think about it. "Ask her to leave?"

Mom laughs out loud at that. "Probably a good idea. But I have another thought. How about telling her that you would appreciate it if she would keep any not-nice thoughts to herself?"

"That might work," I tell her. "But do you

think she will do that?" I am more worried than I want Mom to know.

Mom shakes her head no. "I really don't think she will."

Dad pops his head in the door. "Pizza's here."

"Are you going to sit in on my book club tonight?" Mom asks.

Last week was the first time I have ever missed a book club meeting. And I don't want to miss another one.

"Of course!" I answer. I grab my notepad for taking notes on their great book ideas. And then I follow Mom to the living room to help set up the chairs.

Nothing like spending an hour with a group of people who love books as much as I do. Mom's book club gives me the courage to ask Charlotte to come over Friday.

I see myself standing in front of my house, wearing my green
armor, and carrying my purple shield with the picture of a
unicorn on it. I am armed with a stack of books. I will protect
myself with my belief in reading and books. I will not be afraid
of turning a page. I will keep moving toward the ending. A
good ending is always worth fighting for, no matter what.

On Thursday morning, Siri actually sort of smiles at me. And I smile back. The Shun is a thing of the past. But she doesn't talk to me at lunch, even though I sit with the Unicorns. And she doesn't even clap for me when I spin around as the fairy godmother in the drama club game of the day. I still think I am way too old to be playing princess, but I want to make an effort to be part of the Unicorns. And if they want to play princesses, I guess I can try for them.

"Thanks for eating with us today," Daisy tells me on the way back to the classroom after lunch. "We missed you."

"Maybe not all of you," I grumble with a look toward Siri.

Daisy shrugs. "She's still mad about the book club. She'll get over it."

I shrug too, mimicking Daisy. "Hope so."

★ ★ ★

Friday afternoon, the one and only Charlotte Thomas comes to my house. And I am ready for her. Only she isn't anything like I expected. She is actually sort of nice.

"I like your room," Charlotte says, complimenting me. She is sitting on my floor, petting Abe on the stomach. "And your dog. I wish I had a dog. You are so lucky."

"Thanks," I say as I sit down beside her. "Here are some of my favorite books." I hand her a stack of books. "Some of these were my mom's. She saved them for me."

Charlotte gently picks up *Island of the Blue Dolphins*. She runs her hand over the cover and then opens the book to look at the first page. "I don't have anything from my mom."

I don't know what to say. So I keep my mouth closed. For once, I don't say anything.

"This is beautiful. I wish I could read it," Charlotte confides.

I take the book from her hands and open to the first page. "The first step in learning to read is to love books. You have to want to read them. If you let yourself fall into the story, it will be easier to work through reading the words."

"Thank you for helping me," Charlotte says, shaking her hair out of her eyes. "I've never wanted to read a book as much as I want to read this one."

"I have an extra copy you can borrow," I tell her, pulling a paperback from my bookshelf. "Let's read it out loud together."

And we start on page one.

Charlotte never says one rude word the entire time she is at my house. Actually, when her grandmother picks her up just before my piano lesson, she asks if she can come again next week.

I wave good-bye at the front door. Charlotte waves and holds up *Island of the Blue Dolphins*.

Gram pats me on the shoulder. I didn't realize she was just behind me.

"You did a good thing, pumpkin. A forever kind of thing," she says as she kisses me on the top of my head.

I turn around and close the door behind me. "What do you mean?" I ask.

"Reading is forever. You are giving Charlotte a gift she will have with her the rest of her life."

"I never thought about it that way before," I say. But I guess it's true. Even when Charlotte is all grown up, she will still be able to read.

CHAPTER 16

The Best Ending of All

I only have one thing left to do.

The next week, Mrs. Sablinsky calls me to the front of the Friday morning assembly. And I make an announcement in front of the entire school.

"Hi, I'm Ruby Starr, and I am in Mrs. Sablinsky's fifth-grade class. From now on, every Tuesday will be a Book Club Tuesday. Bring your favorite book to lunch, and find someone to share it with. You can always come and join me. I love all books. Oh, and one more thing, everyone is welcome."

Talking in front of the whole school is harder

than it looks. I breathe out and realize I have been holding my breath. Then I look at Mrs. Sablinsky. She nods and pats me on the shoulder. She even smiles at me, with teeth! And she doesn't sigh once.

I see all my favorite characters in a line. All these characters I admire and love. They are my best friends and my role models. And the most amazing thing of all is that they are all clapping for me. I smile and wave. I know they are proud of me. And the best part is—I am proud of myself.

I walk back to my seat. I see Siri, Jessica, Daisy, and Charlotte. They are clapping for me. Will P and his friends are clapping too. In fact, everyone is clapping. It's just like I imagined, only it's for real. And they are all clapping for me.

Siri runs over to me. She throws her arms around me and hugs me tight. "Best friends always forgive each other, right?" she asks me.

I hug her back. "Always."

★ ★ ★

And the very next Tuesday, Book Club Tuesday, every single lunch bench is full. The Unicorns have a few new members. Charissa and her friends are joining us to read *A Wrinkle in Time*. Charlotte is coming over today after school so I can help her read the first few chapters. She still hasn't told the rest of our friends, but she says she will soon.

I break away from the Unicorns to visit the Polar Bears. I have finished *The Secret Merlin*

Society, and I can't wait to share my favorite parts. The boys are actually talking about the book, and no one is even throwing food or fake vomiting. Will P shows me his socks. They are sky blue with pairs of yellow wings all over them.

"Hero socks," Will tells me, and his eyes get all big behind his glasses. "For you, Ruby. 'Cause you brought everyone together."

I duck my head, because I'm not used to compliments, especially from boys. Not that I like Will P—I mean, like-like. I don't. But still, getting a compliment is kind of embarrassing and amazing at the same time. I also realize something: This story wasn't about Charlotte like I thought it was the day she walked into Room 15. It was about me.

"You are fantastically braver than brave," Will P finishes.

"Thanks, Will," I manage. "I hope I'm still part of the Polar Bears," I add. I don't want to share lunch with them, but I like reading all different types of books, and the Polar Bears choose adventurous stories.

"Absolutely," Will answers.

I move around the yard, checking in with the different groups. Some are reading mysteries, and others are reading books from movies. Mrs. Sablinsky is even sitting out here, instead of inside the teachers' lounge. Four teachers are sitting with her, and they all have books with them. I can't wait to tell my mom that even the teachers have joined in.

It's most possibly the best day of my life. I stand in the middle of the lunch benches and look around. Books have brought everyone together.

And that's when I know exactly who I will be for Halloween. I won't be a character from a book. I will be a book. A book with a green cover and a pink spine and lots and lots of pages.

Because books can change the world.

Acknowledgments

A perpetual thank you to my always fabulous agent Stacey Glick for loving Ruby from the beginning and for always encouraging me to write what is in my heart.

Thank you to my incredible team and partners at Sourcebooks Jabberwocky:

Thank you to my gifted editor Annie Berger for connecting with Ruby and her love of books and for believing in the story I wanted to tell. I am grateful to Elizabeth Boyer and Diane Dannenfeldt for their insightful and thorough editing. Nicole Komasinski created designs that are beyond anything I could have imagined. The immensely talented Jeanine Murch has won my eternal gratitude for the illustrations that have brought Ruby's imagination to life so beautifully. Thank you to Katy Lynch and Alex Yeadon for their hard work and dedication to sharing Ruby with the world through publicity and marketing. I also want to thank Steve Geck, Todd Stocke, and Dominique Raccah for supporting the imperfectly perfect Ruby and for taking this journey with me.

Thank you to my family for their endless support and friendship and for being book crazy people! Thank you to my girls, Ava and Caroline, for being my first and most trusted readers and for always believing in me. And thank you to God for making all things possible.

About the Author

Deborah Lytton writes books for middle grade and young adult readers. She is the author of *Jane in Bloom* and *Silence*. Deborah has a history degree from UCLA and a law degree from Pepperdine University. She lives in Los Angeles, California, with her two daughters and their dog, Faith. For more information about Deborah, visit deborahlytton.com.